Boy Made of Dawn

R. Allen Chappell

DEDICATION

Again, many sincere thanks to those Navajo friends and classmates who provided "grist for the mill." Their insight into Navajo thought and reservation life helped fuel a lifelong interest in their culture, one I had once only observed from the other side of the fence.

Table of Contents

ACKNOWLEDGMENTS

In the grand view of things an author often deludes himself, thinking *he* has written a book. The truth is few books are written without the help of others. From those who do the tendering of ideas and information, to the editing and proofreading, a certain toll is taken on the original work—almost always for the better. I would like to thank all those whose efforts have contributed to "our" book.

Author's Note

In the back pages you will find a small glossary of Navajo words and terms used in the story, the spelling of which may vary somewhat depending on which "expert's" opinion is referenced.

1

The Rescue

Man has always felt most vulnerable in that lonely netherworld between darkness and dawn. Often it is then death takes the sick and weak. They give up finally, unable to bear the weight of another day. A person may—not knowing why—suddenly awaken, if only for an instant, to assure himself all is well.

Charlie Yazzie woke that morning in the darkness with just such a feeling.

It was now late afternoon, and hunger was finally getting the best of him. In old Navajo when one was hungry he said, "Hunger is hurting me." Hunger was hurting Charlie now.

On his way back from Blanding—entering Bluff, Utah, he was at the very northern edge of the reservation. Legal Services had sent him to take a follow-up deposition in a domestic violence case, one originating on the Navajo reservation. It had been a wasted trip. No one at the rural address knew the plaintiff or where she might be found. Either the contact information had been wrongly transcribed, or there was a mix-up in the case files.

The only cafe in the town was nearly deserted. The girl who brought the menu and ice water seemed out of sorts, as though doing him a favor. He thought she might be *Ute*, maybe from the old *Ute* land allotments just up the road. It was just a hunch. She might as easily have been *Piute*. Charlie knew, early on, the government had scattered the few *Piute* in this area among the *Ute,* thinking them the same people. They later found this was not the case, but by that time it was too late, and they actually were pretty much the same people.

"What's good for dinner?" he asked with a smile.

She studied him for a moment, taking in the fresh shirt, pressed jeans, and shiny boots. She had watched him pull up in the new Chevrolet truck with the tribal emblem on the side. "Well, there's the Navajo taco platter," she said with a slight smirk, jabbing her finger at the number on the menu. "These people around here seem to like it." She did not smile when she said this.

He nodded, purposely taking his time now with the menu, examining it as a condemned man might contemplate his last meal. The girl, who was dark skinned and had a twitch in her left eye, tapped her foot, pencil poised. There was always this little thing between Navajo and the *Ute.* It had been going on a very long time.

It was *Ute* scouts who led Kit Carson in his roundup of the Navajo, causing their long walk to eastern New Mexico and interminable incarceration at Bosque Redondo. One hundred and fifty years later, it was still a sore subject, often vilified as the most horrifying event in Navajo history.

The Navajo taco platter actually sounded pretty good, but he would not give this rude girl the satisfaction.

"I'll have the chicken-fried steak," he said pointing at it, "with fries and extra gravy…and make that white gravy!" He wanted her to know he wasn't from around there.

Still, the smirk played at the corner of her mouth. "Salad dressing?"

"Honey mustard…if you've got it." He refused to be played.

"We got it," she declared with a curt bob of her head. "We don't get much call for it…but we got it."

"I'll have that dressing on the side, please," he added firmly.

She grimaced, writing the notation so hard she broke the pencil lead. She glared at the pencil then shot Charlie a hard look. "It'll be right out." She moved to the order window where he was pleased to see two older white women, with their hair in nets, in charge of the kitchen. He watched carefully to see she didn't do anything to his food, but she knew better.

Halfway through his dinner (which was surprisingly good) an older, rough-looking man came in and seated himself at the counter across the aisle from Charlie's table. He was a big man for an Indian. The *Ute* girl moved quickly down the counter, speaking to him in a fashion indicating a certain familiarity. They whispered for a few minutes, the man turning on his stool a time or two, looking over at Charlie. Finally, he rose and came over to the table. "My name is Hiram Buck." He didn't offer his hand. "My niece over there says that's your truck outside. Are you the law?"

Charlie put down his fork and looked the man over, finally nodding. "In a way I suppose you could say I am. I'm with Navajo Nation Legal Services." Charlie took a card from his shirt pocket and passed it to him. "Is there something I can help you with?"

"It's not me that needs help." The man looked briefly at the card. "But there's a little boy out in the canyons who I think might. I was out there today gathering some stray stock and ran across him up in an old *Anasazi* ruin back in the canyons. He can't be more than five or six years old. He ran and hid in the rocks when he saw I spotted him. My cows was getting away, and by time I had them settled he had just disappeared! He's still up there somewhere I expect, but damned if I could find him. Anyway, I guess someone should go up there before something happens to him." He raised his right hand as though swearing to the veracity of his statement. "There was no sign of anyone else around. I yelled and hollered but didn't get no answer." The man was becoming agitated. "It is five or six miles from the nearest road. I just can't figure out why he might be up there all alone, that's all. No one lives up that way that I know of." He paused for a moment and looked Charlie directly in the eye. "There are a couple hours of daylight left. If you want me to, I can take you back up there or at least to the corrals where I left the stock. I left my horse up there too. You could use him to ride in if you wanted to. I'll come back for the horse in the morning. I just think some kind of law should go up there and see what's what!" The man stopped to catch his breath, watching intently to see what effect all this talk might be having on Charlie.

Charlie, for his part, didn't quite know what to make of it. He suspected there was a logical explanation for the boy being out there and thought it most likely someone was looking after him. There was little doubt, however, that this man was genuinely concerned.

The man spoke again, slowly this time, as though he thought Charlie might not understand what he was saying. "My Niece over there," indicating the waitress with a nod of his head, "she says the local law had to take his wife to the hospital in Cortez a couple of hours ago, and there's probably no one here in town can do anything. I think something ought to be done right now while there's still enough daylight to get back up there!"

Charlie pondered this for only a moment before putting some bills on the table. "Let's go," he said softly.

As though on signal, the man's niece took two bottles of water from the cooler and slid an apple pie into a cardboard box. She passed them to her uncle, who handed them to Charlie. "It might be a long night," was all he said.

~~~~~~~

Hiram Buck knew the rutted roads like they were part of his DNA, which they probably were. Some think the *Ute* have been in that country longer than anyone—even the *Anasazi*. They were a desperately poor people in the beginning, living in small isolated family bands. They had posed little threat to those who came after, at least until much later when they got a few horses away from the Spaniards. They were the first Indians to have horses. It was not long before they were a force to be reckoned with.

Not many knew it, but Charlie had always held an interest in the pre-history of the Four Corners and its people. The University of New Mexico was a Mecca for some of the foremost scholars in the field, and he had taken classes from some of the best. More than one had tried to convince him to switch his major from law. He, however, thought he could do more good in the future than the past. He was learning of late that the two were often intertwined.

Charlie was aware many of the indigenous peoples of an area often go back to a shared gene pool. In early days there was much raiding and taking of women and children. It is sometimes difficult for latter-day ethnologists to keep the various groups separated by genetic makeup alone.

The Navajo adopted some of their culture from the ancient Pueblo peoples. Weaving and pottery making, along with rudimentary farming, were all thought to have been acquired from the Pueblos. After the introduction of sheep by the Spaniards, the Navajo took the craft of weaving to a new level. Their pottery, on the other hand, never seemed to advance beyond a plain cooking ware.

A major point of differentiation among the groups was their language rootstock affiliation: *Athabaskan* for the Navajo/Apache, *Shoshonean* for the *Ute*, and several unrelated languages for the various Pueblo peoples. No one was really certain where some of those early Pueblo people came from, though there were plenty of theories.

Some authorities believe the *Ute* may have descended directly from the early Paleo-Indian whose bones and spear points litter the Southwest—some as old as ten thousand years or more. The *Ute* had been rubbing elbows with the Navajo and their Apache cousins for nearly a thousand years. By the latter portion of that time, the three peoples shared a number of cultural traits. Charlie knew the Navajo's genetic diversity might well be one reason they were one of the few modern tribes increasing in number.

~~~~~~~

It was all Charlie could do to keep up with Hiram Buck, even with the new truck. He tried the two-way radio several times in hopes of raising someone back at dispatch. He wanted to relay his change of plans, but, as often was the case in that country, the iron-bearing cliffs deflected the signal, leaving only static and distant garbled bits and snatches of voices.

There was only about an hour of light left when they reached the trailhead. Hiram's dilapidated stock trailer was backed up to the loading chute. Three cows lounged in the weathered cedar corrals. He had tied his horse on the shady side of the trailer where there were scattered flakes of hay on the ground. Hiram had removed the saddle from the horse before leaving, which told Charlie he had not been sure when he would return. Hiram backed his truck up to the trailer and lowered the hitch onto the ball then dragged his saddle from the back of the old pickup. Charlie, meanwhile, pulled on a Levi's jacket and grabbed a blanket from the back seat of his Chevy. He also retrieved his revolver from the glove box and a folding knife he thought might come in handy. Hiram watched him out of the corner of his eye as he brought the horse around and bridled it. He left the halter and lead rope under the bridle, as is usual in that country. The saddle had a set of cheap canvas bags behind the cantle, the sort of tack auctioned off at a sale-barn before they settle on the more serious business of running the stock through.

Hiram straightened the blanket for Charlie as he hefted the saddle on and cinched it up tight, causing the gelding to groan. This horse was full of hay, and he knew the cinch would loosen quickly enough. He didn't want to stop and tighten it again if the trail got rough, and the trails in this country always got rough. Both men smiled when Charlie put the pie box in the saddlebag—that pie was in for a ride. He put the water bottles in the opposite saddlebag, tied his blanket roll over them, and was pretty much ready to go. Hiram pointed up the left fork of the trail and moved his chin in the direction of the corralled cows. "Those girls have to be at the sale barn in Cortez early in the morning…I can't afford not to have them there."

Charlie nodded and swung up on the horse with a wave of his arm to Hiram, who was already moving to load the cows.

All Charlie had to do was follow this horse's tracks back up the canyon. He thought he could make it before darkness covered the trail, provided it was no farther than Hiram Buck had said. Tall, black thunderheads gathered like a war party in the Northwest, and he eyed them with a grim resignation.

He had to kick-start the horse, who had it in mind to stay with the cows and Hiram. The gelding was none too happy to be headed back up the trail this late in the day, and with a stranger to boot. It was a good, stout horse. The *Ute* have always kept good horses.

The trail was steep and rocky for the first mile or so, and Charlie had to stop and let the horse blow at the first switchback. Once out of sight of the trailhead, the gelding put his head down, getting his mind right. Charlie wondered if Hiram might want to sell this gelding. He had been thinking of getting a horse for some time. Some believe the *Ute* are a bit rough in their horse training, but you can count on their horses to do what they are asked to do, and you don't have to ask them twice. Charlie noticed several sets of fresh horse tracks on the trail, but only old signs of cattle. Hiram must have driven his cows down the creek bed. The trail wound on up the canyon, often clinging to the side of the cliff in a rather alarming manner.

He was nearly running out of daylight when he finally urged the sorrel gelding up the cedar slope that hid the ruins. It was a small site, probably no more than ten or twelve rooms, including a couple of small granaries against the back wall. Charlie had helped do volunteer fieldwork on several sites just like it at the university. He could see by the dark line of moss at the rear of the declivity that there was a seep with enough water for a thirsty boy.

Charlie knew instinctively it would do no good to try to call the boy out in the dark. If the child had run from Hiram in the light of day, he would certainly do the same with him in the darkness. He also did not relish the thought of a precarious ride back down the canyon in the black of night. He quietly tied the gelding in the scrub oak near the ruin, rolling out his blanket in the soft duff under a juniper at the edge of the rocky walls. The boy would be watching now. Charlie hoped he would take some comfort from another human nearby. The clouds rolled in about midnight, and there was quite a display of lightning and thunder, but only a few drops of rain. There would be fear in the boy now, leaving him worn out by morning. Maybe then he would be ready to come out of hiding.

Charlie Yazzie rolled over in his blanket, turning on one side to peer at the ruins through the shadowy darkness of pre-dawn. Death was never far away for these ancient people, and now after a thousand years it again seemed to hover in the shadows.

The boy was there. Charlie could sense it. He knew time was not on his side. Another Navajo might not have lingered through a long, cold night at the edge of the ruined dwellings. Charlie Yazzie's years at government boarding school and then university had stripped away superstitious fear of the dead—or nearly so.

There was only a fine line of gray on the eastern mesas when Charlie shook off his blanket in the chill night air. He silently worked his way closer to the hollow walls, settling himself on the crumbling edge of the *kiva* to await the dawn.

As first light touched the ruins, a small, quavering voice wafted up from the depths of the overhang. The almost indiscernible words were in Navajo—it was the *Dinè* blessing song sung to greet the day. Charlie's grandmother had taught him this same song as a child. This boy had been brought up by someone who still believed in the Beauty Way. It was obvious now he was Navajo. Charlie stood and raised his voice above the breeze, singing along with the boy who faltered momentarily then picked up the thread of the last verse:

> Beauty above me
> Beauty below me
> Beauty all around me
> I walk in beauty

The song is sometimes sung with slightly different words in the beginning, but always, the last verse is the same, and the little voice became stronger at the end. The boy cautiously emerged from the blackness at the back of the ruins and stood in the jumble of rocks and broken walls. Charlie averted his eyes as one would when dealing with a wild animal. Not looking directly at the boy, he retrieved the pie box and water bottles from the saddlebags. As he turned, he saw the child had come closer, standing in the warm halo of a breaking dawn. There was a glow about him as though he were made of dawn. He was a small boy for his age, which appeared to be about what Hiram Buck had reported. He was dirty (with the dust of the ruins in his hair) thin and hollow eyed. *Dinè* boys are born tough, capable of enduring physical hardship at a very young age—in olden times this endurance had been a prerequisite for survival.

"Da dichin' ninizen?" Charlie asked, holding out the pie box with its jumbled contents. The boy gave a slight nod of his head and inched forward to take a handful of the wrecked apple pie. Still, he said nothing, and Charlie did not push him to talk. They

ate silently, not looking at one another, and drank the water. Charlie re-saddled the horse as he watched the boy finish the crumbs. "Are your people nearby?" he asked in Navajo. The boy shook his head indicating they were not. Charlie mounted the horse and offered the boy a hand up; he did not hesitate but swung up behind in silence.

As they rode down the shadowed canyon trail in the cool of early morning, Charlie was glad the boy was at least wearing a heavy sweatshirt. The offer of his jacket had been refused. The *Ute* horse cautiously picked his way down a particularly rough stretch. As is often the case, the trail was more treacherous going down than coming up. Again, it occurred to Charlie what a fine horse this was. Not so much for looks, but it had good sense and was broke for anyone who could sit up straight and ride. They eased their way down toward a trickle of water meandering through a thin band of young cottonwoods. The horse had not drunk that morning, and Charlie let him leave the main trail and follow a well-beaten path to the stream. He could see by the tracks that this horse had watered there the previous day.

The boy slid off, and Charlie dismounted and loosened the girth, lowering the reins so the horse might drink his fill; it might be his last drink that day. The boy moved downstream to a little patch of oak brush to relieve himself, and Charlie smiled at this bit of backcountry etiquette from one so young. He pulled the empty water bottles from the saddlebags, intending to fill them from the clear pool beside the horse. As he went down on one knee and leaned over to fill the bottles, the horse suddenly tossed his head and whinnied, jerking back on the reins, causing Charlie to lose his balance and sprawl backwards in the tall grass. It was at that instant a rifle shot exploded—a geyser of water erupting just where Charlie had knelt the moment before. Instinctively, he rolled sideways into the cover of the willows and called for the boy to get down. As the shot echoed down the canyon, he momentarily lost track of the boy. The horse had jerked loose and now, confused, stepped forward into the water; he did not bolt but stood transfixed, staring across the narrow canyon. He was blocking Charlie's view but offered enough cover to crawl toward the boy. They met behind a large boulder that lay half in the stream. Charlie pulled the boy to him, shielding him with his own body. His pistol was out of the shoulder holster, and he held it out away from the boy, who was shivering now. Charlie himself was trembling and placed the boy beside him, back against the rock, his arm still around him. That shot had come from a good distance, and he knew his .38 would not have the range to confront this person, who was obviously a very good shot. That horse had saved his life, to his way of thinking. After a few minutes of numbing silence, Charlie could hear the faint, far-off metallic clatter of a shod horse's hooves on slick rock.

Maybe the shooter thought Charlie had been hit when he was thrown backwards; or maybe he just figured he had missed his chance and best get away while he could; or maybe the shooter's horse had run off without him, and he was up there waiting for another shot. He looked over at the boy, who gave a little half-grin and shrugged his shoulders. This made Charlie smile. This boy would do well someday, given half a chance.

Charlie waited as long as he could stand it and then indicated to the boy that he should stay put. He rolled sideways into the oak brush for a view of the rim without being seen. He studied the area he thought the shot had come from and noted, directly across from them, an old, fallen spruce log well out on the otherwise bare sandstone point. It was only about two hundred yards as the crow flies—the canyon narrowed that much at this point. Perfect place for an ambush for someone who knew how to shoot, he thought. After a few more minutes, he cautiously stood up, ready to hit the dirt at the first sign of movement. Keeping an eye on the rim, he eased over and picked up the reins to the horse. It had lowered its head and was now calmly cropping grass. Charlie thought this was the kind of horse a man might be able to shoot off of—should the need arise. His grandfather had often cautioned him there was never any justification for shooting off a horse; there were very few that would stand for it. He tightened the cinch and, after another careful look around, called to the boy, who rose up and came over, ready to clamber back aboard.

Back on the trail, Charlie's mind raced as he searched every tree and boulder ahead. He couldn't help but notice a number of horse tracks coming and going on this trail, both shod and unshod. He studied the tracks with the skill earned following run-off stock as a boy. The sign was clear to him once he had let his mind return to that time when being a tracker was something of value. Again, it struck him as odd that there were no fresh cow tracks, and he pondered the possibilities. A shadow of trepidation made for a much slower return, though the horse was now champing at the bit, anxious to be fed, and possibly looking forward to a little equine company. No matter the training, a horse is a herd animal, a trait any real horseman keeps always in the front of his mind. As they neared the trailhead, Charlie scanned the path ahead, halting occasionally to survey the terrain.

He could sense the boy grow nervous again, felt him flinch and hold tight as the horse nickered and shook himself at the sight of the corrals. Something bad had happened here, and it was running through the boys mind. He still had not spoken a word. There would be plenty of time for that later; now, he needed to get this boy back to town.

He also needed to call Sue Hanagarni, who he had promised to meet for breakfast this morning. Shiprock and the Dinè Bikeyah Cafe were still some hours down the road.

He saw Hiram had left a couple of flakes of hay for the horse. The *Ute* would probably be back for it after he finished at the sale-barn in Cortez. Hiram Buck had gone to a lot of trouble for this boy. Charlie intended to let him know later how it all turned out.

The boy slid off the horse and immediately went to open the corral gate for Charlie—he had obviously spent time around stock and was anxious to pitch in and help. Charlie liked this boy. He could see a lot of himself in him when he was young. They stashed the tack out of sight behind the corral and sat in the pickup truck for a few minutes while Charlie once again tried, unsuccessfully, to reach someone on the radio. He noticed the boy, out of the corner of his eye, entranced by the truck's multi-lighted instrument panel and radio controls. The boy was enumerating each of them with a tentative forefinger as though trying to understand their function. Most Indian boys love pickup trucks as their forefathers loved horses. They are the path to being a man, they think.

Charlie took the cutoff. When he hit the flats out of Aneth, he radioed the switchboard and had the operator forward a message to

Sue Hanagarni: they had best meet for lunch instead of breakfast. They had known one another since boarding school and had worked together in Legal Services for two years now. Sue was an easygoing girl, but he knew he would have some explaining to do. He thought he would ask Sue to marry him at some point.

Charlie turned on 160 to Teec Nos Pos then dropped down on 64 toward Shiprock. As the miles slipped by, he once or twice tried to engage the boy in conversation, first in English and then Navajo, but could get no more than a nod or shake of his head in return. There was something hauntingly familiar about this boy he could not get out of his head. Maybe it was because he had been much the same himself as a youngster.

They had to pass right by his place on the way into town. He thought they had time to clean up a bit and maybe give the boy's clothes a quick wash on half cycle. The clothes were still a bit damp when they left, but it was warm out, and there was no help for it. Sue would be waiting at the Dinè Bikeyah—and she wouldn't wait long.

When they pulled up to the restaurant, her old Datsun pickup was in the parking lot right next to the entrance, which meant she had arrived early before the Saturday lunch crowd. The boy looked better cleaned up—his hair slicked down with a little Wildroot Cream Oil that Charlie kept for his cowlick when it acted up. The boy was not used to being all spruced up. He kept looking at his image in the truck's side mirror; he gave no sign he liked what he saw.

They spotted Sue at a far table by a window and came up on her while she studied the menu. When she looked up, she at first did not see the child standing slightly behind Charlie.

"Well, it's about ti..." Her greeting trailed off as she saw the boy peeking out from behind him. The boy shrugged his shoulders at the surprised look on her face.

"This is...well, I don't know who he is," Charlie offered, nudging the boy forward.

Sue smiled. "What! Did he follow you home?" She turned the smile on the boy. "What's your name, fella?" The boy dropped his head and did not answer. "Oh, a shy guy, huh? Well, that's all right. I like the strong, silent type...so unlike some people I know," she said casting Charlie a sideways glance, but still smiling.

"What? I'm strong!" Charlie flexed his biceps. He eased the boy into the booth ahead of him and moved one of the silverware packets over in front of him. "I'll bet you're hungry again, huh?"

Sue thought the boy awfully thin. "When did he eat last?"

"Well, he had a scrambled apple pie for breakfast about daylight, but that's about it. I don't think he's had a whole lot to eat lately."

Sue raised her eyebrows. "Whole apple pie, huh? That ought to put some meat on his bones."

Charlie laughed. "I helped him with the pie...but you'd be surprised."

"I'll bet," Sue grinned back. She had already selected lunch so passed him the menu. She was glad to see Charlie and wanted him to know it. She touched his hand across the table. "Does he talk at all?" she asked.

"No, but he can sing a blue streak...when he wants too." He turned to the boy. "What's it going to be, guy?" The boy said nothing. "How about a big cheese burger and some fries with ketchup?" The boy looked down at the table, but a hint of a smile crossed his lips.

After the waitress took their orders, Charlie launched into the story of how he had come by the boy, who stared out the window rather than see the sad look on Sue's face as she listened. Charlie left out the part about the shooting. The food came, and the boy tucked away his with a will. Charlie unwrapped the silverware for him, but the boy—engrossed in the food—paid no attention. "I was surprised he came to me." Charlie said around a mouthful of burger. "Him not knowing me and all."

The boy turned and looked at Charlie. "I know you," he said softly. "You are Thomas Begay's friend!"

Charlie spluttered and almost dropped his fork. He cocked his head at the boy. "How do you know Thomas Begay?" he said forgetting to speak Navajo. And then it hit him. "And I know who you are too now, *atsili*!" He put his fork down and looked across the table at Sue, who was staring open-mouthed at them. "This is Sally Klee's boy from over by Farmington. You remember, Thomas Begay's "friend" from the Greyhorse case last fall!"

Sue raised her eyebrows, staring at the boy, and then nodded. "I remember."

"Well, let's finish lunch," he said with a quick glance at Sue, who nodded.

Charlie thought it best to let the thing lie; this would be something best left alone until Thomas Begay was present. The bright spot was, the boy would not now have to be turned over to Social Services—not just yet anyway.

In the parking lot Charlie had the boy stay in the truck while he and Sue stepped away to talk.

"Busy this afternoon?" he asked.

She shook her head.

"Good. Want to take a ride out to Thomas's? I think we need to have a little chat. I'm wondering now where Sally and this boy's sister are."

Sue was up for it, and the boy scooted right over when she got in the truck.

Thomas and Lucy Tallwoman had become good friends since the Greyhorse affair. The four of them now occasionally met in town for dinner at Denny's or sometimes had cookouts at Lucy's place. Sue and Charlie had both known Thomas since boarding school in Aztec and had been close; then Charlie went away to law school, and Thomas's drinking took control of his life. Thomas did not drink now. Lucy Tallwoman had become a friend of Sue's, and on the way out to her camp, Sue caught Charlie's eye. Looking over the boy's head, she silently mouthed the question, "Does Lucy know about this boy?"

Charlie mirrored her quizzical expression and shrugged his shoulders. He had never discussed the matter with Thomas beyond the time Thomas had admitted the boy and his sister were his. It had happened long before he had known Lucy Tallwoman; he did not think Thomas would have told her.

Charlie's mind ranged back to that autumn afternoon when he and Thomas had gone out to Sally Klee's *hogan* under the bluffs outside Farmington. They had been looking for her half-brother Freddy Chee but wound up with more than they bargained for, including a briefcase full of evidence that proved instrumental in bringing down a number of very important people—people who would be coming to trial soon. He remembered Sally as a small, thin young woman who spoke English like his grandmother. She was probably no more than twenty-five years old at the time. He recalled her half-brother Freddy Chee had earlier given her a beating to insure her silence. Still, she had risked telling Thomas what she knew of Freddie's part in the matter. She had also told him she was leaving that place and going to live with her cousins. Charlie doubted she ever moved back to that old *hogan.* Freddie had died a violent and lonely death there. His *chindi* would still be trapped in that *Hogan*—and the *chindi* of a *yeenaaldiooshii* is not to be trifled with. Neither she nor any other Navajo would ever live in that *hogan* again.

~~~~~~~

Lucy Tallwoman's old father Paul T'Sosi was just bringing the sheep down from the cedar hills behind the *hogan* when they pulled up in the yard. The boy perked up immediately and watched intently through the windshield as the dog worked the sheep into the corrals. He glanced at Charlie and smiled. It seemed plain the boy had the primal instinct to follow the herds—it was part of who he was.

The old man waved but finished with the sheep before coming over. *"Ya' eh t'eeh,"* he called even before reaching the truck. Charlie heard the old man had not been well these last few weeks, but he looked fine now. He was smiling as he patted the hood of the new Chevy. "This is more like it," he grinned. "Legal Services is finally stepping up, huh."

Charlie laughed and pointed to the blue Dodge truck next to the *hogan.* "I see you finally got another truck too!" He knew it was really Lucy's truck, but the polite thing was to acknowledge the old man's part in the thing.

"Oh, Thomas Begay got tired of hay-wiring that old one back together, I guess. He picked it out. He just had to have a diesel. I don't know where he plans to plug it in this winter; we can't run the generator all night just so this truck will start." He had slipped in the part about their having a new generator as an indicator of how well they were doing. Paul had come up to the window now, and Charlie could see he truly wasn't pleased with Thomas's choice of a truck.

"The salesman told us it would pull a *hogan* off its foundation...going uphill...into the wind!" He spit in the dust. "I don't know why anyone would want to pull their *hogan* off its foundation," and then as an afterthought, "anyways, *hogans* don't even have foundations." They both laughed at this, and the old man shook his head. "That Thomas," he grinned. "At least he's not drinking anymore, and he's making a little money right along, too."

Charlie nodded. "That's good!" There really wasn't much more he could say about that.

Sue peeked around Charlie and waved at the old man. "Hi there! The sheep are looking good! Is Lucy still working on the *Ye'i* blanket?"

Paul liked Sue and couldn't understand why she and Charlie hadn't gotten married yet; they were together all the time, and he liked to tease them about it whenever he got the chance. "She's still working on it. I expect that's what she's doing right now. At least she was when I left with the sheep this morning." Paul turned his attention to the boy between them. "Who's that little guy?"

"That's what we're about to find out, I hope. Is Thomas around?"

"Should be up by now. He had to work most of last night for the road crew on a washout up the road."

The boy perked up at the mention of Thomas's name. "Thomas," he whispered to himself, but no one heard.

Charlie and Sue got out of the truck, leaving the boy in the front seat watching them, and with the old man trailing behind, slowly made their way up to the *hogan*. They figured Lucy Tallwoman already knew they were there but wanted to give her a few minutes. Spur-of-the-moment visits were the norm in this country, but Sue knew Lucy would appreciate at least a few minutes.

Thomas Begay appeared at the open door, bleary-eyed and tired looking, to welcome them. He held a cup of coffee in one hand and flipped his long hair out of his eyes with the other. Charlie moved forward. "Sorry to spring this on you, *hastiin,* but we didn't know what else to do." Charlie indicated the Chevy with a twist of his head.

"Spring what?" Thomas looked from one to the other of them. "What are you talking about?"

The boy, arms folded on the dashboard, stared silently out the windshield at Thomas. When Thomas glanced over at the truck, he calmly placed his coffee cup down on the water barrel by the door and moved past them to the Chevy. The others fell silent and looked away as he opened the door and lifted the little boy out, standing him on the ground and straightening his shirt. Together, the two of them walked toward the corrals, Thomas speaking softly in Navajo and the boy nodding his head from time to time.

Lucy came to the door smiling at her unexpected guests. "This is a nice surprise..." She stopped in midsentence as she saw Thomas and the boy watching the sheep together. Her face clouded for an instant, but she immediately regained her composure, motioning everyone into the *hogan.*

Sue instantly took up the slack by exclaiming loudly over the weaving loom set up inside the door, "Oh, Lucy! It's nearly done. How do you do it? I thought it would take forever!" As Lucy and Sue examined the blanket in its final stages of weaving, Lucy showed her the tiny imperfection purposely woven into the warp of one corner. Sue knew this almost imperceptible thread at the lower corner of the blanket was done to allow the weavers spirit to escape the piece, insuring she could detach her spirit from it and let it go. It was thought the weaver became part of the piece during the creation. It was a tradition common in most Navajo art.

The two men seated themselves at the table. "Is that Thomas's boy?" the old man asked Charlie in a low voice. "I've heard the rumors before, but there are so many about Thomas I never know which ones to believe anymore."

Charlie shifted uncomfortably in his chair and did not meet the old man's gaze. "I guess so," he managed finally.

The old man shook his head. "That Thomas..." His voice trailed off as he looked to his daughter caught up in conversation with Sue. She cast an occasional sideways glance out the little window at the corrals. "She knows all about it." He answered Charlie's unasked question by saying, "Has for several years now. It happened way before they met, I guess…seems like it is just one thing after another with Thomas." He frowned when he said this and stared hard at the door.

Charlie nodded and looked away again. "There's a girl too, you know…somewhere. At least I hope there still is." He could see Sue and Lucy's talk had turned serious, and he suspected Sue was telling how they had come to have the boy. He explained to Paul T'Sosi what had transpired up in the canyons, again leaving out the part about the shooting.

"Well, it's a hell of a thing to treat a little boy like that." And that was all the old man said.

When Thomas, carrying his cup and looking distracted, finally came in, everyone was seated around the table having coffee and discussing the Ye'i blanket.

"The boy's playing with the dog…That dog has never been around no kids, so I thought he might bite him, but he didn't…at least not yet." Thomas smiled and looked around the table. "His name is Caleb. He's six years old. He's never been to school so far. He knows a little English, but not much."

Lucy moved to fill his cup with the last of the breakfast coffee from the big enamelware pot. She did not look directly at him but touched his hand as she withdrew to her seat.

Charlie cleared his throat. "Where's his mother and sister…and what was he doing up in the canyons by himself?

"I don't know all the answers just yet. He doesn't want to talk about it. I think whoever did this threatened him not to talk. I figure I'd best give him a little while. He's worn out. He hasn't had it easy, that's for sure." And then he said thoughtfully, "It's been quite a long time since I last seen him."

Charlie again had to retell as much of the story for Thomas as he thought wise and wound up saying, "He seems pretty smart for only six. He ought to be in school."

"He's six alright. His sister is seven, and he told me she don't go to school, neither." Thomas looked at Lucy when he said this.

Sue spoke up then. "Kind of hard to keep kids out of school these days without people knowing about it, isn't it."

"Not where *they* live it isn't," Thomas said quietly.

Paul T'Sosi studied his cup. "Well, it was quite a coincidence,

Charlie being the one to run across him and all."

"If it was a coincidence," Thomas frowned.

Charlie got the fleeting impression the boy might have let slip more than Thomas was letting on but let it pass. He knew Thomas would fill him in at some point when they could talk.

"Do you want us to take him to Social Services until this is sorted out," Charlie asked looking at Thomas.

"No!" Lucy declared, suddenly standing and speaking in a clear, firm voice. "We will keep him right here till we see what's going on, and where his sister is."

Charlie was not surprised at this but still felt relieved and nodded at Lucy, who looked away.

"I expect school's out for the summer now anyway," the old man said looking at Thomas. "The boy can help me with the sheep 'til we see what's what. That boy seems to like the idea of herding sheep anyway."

Sue looked at Lucy. "I'm off for the next few days. Maybe we could meet up in town tomorrow and find him some more clothes before his ass starts hanging out of those he's wearing." Sue was a straight talker and cared little what people might think about it. That was one of the reasons people liked her—you always knew where you stood with Sue Hanagarni.

2

The Uncle

On the way back into town, Charlie, deep in thought, paid only slight attention to Sue's running on about how proud she was of Lucy offering to care for Caleb and all. Sue thought it declared right up front, for everyone to see, that Lucy stood by Thomas in this thing.

What was bothering Charlie was Thomas's off-hand statement that Charlie's involvement might not be "coincidence." He was beginning to have some niggling little doubts about it himself. He figured he ought to file a report on the entire incident but decided Monday would be soon enough. He pulled up to the Dinè Bikeyah Café where they had left Sue's Datsun. They sat in the Chevy talking until Sue said she had to go home and fix dinner for her parents. She asked if he'd like to join them, but he declined, saying he still needed to write up a case report on the domestic violence assignment.

Sue was the one who allocated the daily work schedule in their office, and he was now reminded to ask how it had come about that he had been the one chosen to go to Blanding. She thought a minute and said, "It was Pete Fish got the original call. Said you should go. Thought it would give you a chance to get out of the office and get some fresh air."

"Hmm," was all Charlie managed. Pete Fish, Sue's old suitor, had been tenacious in his attentions towards her even after Charlie entered the picture. He was still office manager and continued to spend as much time with Sue as possible. Charlie didn't like it.

~~~~~~~~

When he pulled back up to his government duplex, he found the blue Dodge already waiting in his parking space; he pulled in behind it and got out. The wind was picking up, and the usual assorted parking-lot trash was scudding along before it. Charlie really didn't even see it anymore. It was simply a by-product of reservation living. Thomas was out of the truck by the time he reached the Dodge. "I guess we better talk," he said.

Inside, Thomas seated himself at the kitchen table, and Charlie went to the fridge. "You want a bee...err, soda?" He caught himself. "I've got lemon-lime, grape, or cola"

"Grape's good." Thomas was watching intently out the kitchen window at some boys playing baseball in the field behind the apartments. The field was on a broad, elevated bench behind the complex and could easily be seen from the window, even when sitting down. "You got a lot of kids in this neighborhood, huh?"

"I guess so." Charlie sat down but intended to let Thomas do the talking.

Thomas took a long drink of his soda and fiddled with the pop-top tab until he managed to break it off, giving himself a small cut. He immediately stuck the finger in his mouth then examined the cut minutely before looking over at Charlie. "You remember that night up at Sally's place when she told us she was leaving...going to live with her cousins?"

"Yes, I just mentioned that to Sue this morning."

"Those cousins live up there around Cortez. Sally's mother was raised up there. She was *Ute.*" Thomas pronounced the name "*Yu'ta*" like the old people of that tribe. "She was married to a

Navajo. She died when Sally was still little, so her *Ute* aunts raised her along with her cousins. They never paid no attention to her Navajo blood."

Charlie was having a hard time keeping up with Sally Klee's family tree but knew that Thomas himself was perched on one of those limbs as he was a cousin of Freddie Chee. "Uh...so that means you were related to Sally?"

"I guess so. Distant cousin maybe. She claimed her *Ute* family. Clan really never came up until years later. The thing I'm getting at is that Caleb says it was one of the cousins who took him out there and left him in the canyons." He gazed out the window again. "They said someone would come back for him later...and would kill him and his sister if he ever talked about it.

Charlie mulled this over. "Sally's on the prosecution's witness list for the Greyhorse trial...and for that matter, so are we!" He hesitated. "So Caleb doesn't know where his sister and mother are?"

"No, he hasn't seen them in awhile. He was staying with another aunt because there wasn't room enough for everyone where his mother was. It was all women and girls over there, anyway, he said...other than an uncle...Said he was kind of mean. He didn't like him." He watched Charlie's face. "That uncle is Hiram Buck."

Charlie let that sink in a moment and then shook his head. "I must be an idiot," he murmured, brushing a crumb from the checkered plastic tablecloth.

"Maybe, but there was no way you could have known." He threw his hands in the air. "How did they know you would be up there? How did they know you would stop at that cafe? It seems to me there were several coincidences in a row—all of them long shots!" He stood and gazed out the window at the children playing baseball and murmured absentmindedly, "I wonder if Caleb knows how to play baseball."

"You weren't around those kids much, huh?"

"I don't really know. I was drunk most of the time back then. He reexamined the tiny cut on his finger. "Sally didn't want me around them like that. Freddie finally told me he was going to have to kill me if I didn't stop coming around. I could see he meant what he said too. I don't have to tell you what kind of person Freddie was. He was doing some "business" out there at Sally's place and said he didn't need a drunk hanging around seeing stuff he shouldn't." He sighed, watching the game. "I always liked baseball."

Charlie finally got around to telling him about the shooting that morning. "Did the boy say anything to you?"

Thomas was taken aback. "No! He didn't."

"That boy knows how to keep a secret. I asked him not to say anything about it. I told him it was probably just a hunter shooting at some game, and we shouldn't worry everyone with it." Charlie nodded his head at Thomas. "That's quite a boy you've got there."

Thomas passed a hand over his face and nodded. "So, are you saying someone might try to kill everyone on that witness list? That's a lot of killing."

"No, I don't think so. Whoever it is won't try for everyone. You and I are the primary witnesses...along with Sally Klee." He finished his drink in one long gulp and looked at Thomas. "Just keep your eyes open—that's all I'm saying!"

"Sounds to me like we ought to go up there and talk to Sally's cousins. I want to find my daughter before something happens to her...like happened to Caleb...or worse. Those people up there still live like it's the olden times—eye for an eye. I don't think they are smart enough to set up this thing that happened to you, though. They are more of the 'ride-in and shoot'em-up type', if you know what I mean."

"No, someone else is behind this, manipulating and paying them to be a part of it. The question is who?" Charlie rubbed his chin and squinted at the clock over the refrigerator. "How about I pick you up about daylight in the morning, and we make a little circle up through that country and talk to a few people. Someone up there knows where Sally and the girl are."

"Better bring some camp gear and food; hospitality may be a little scarce up there."

Charlie thought that a good idea. "In the meantime I'll poke around and see what I can find out. Sally was supposed to leave her forwarding address with the prosecutor's office before she moved. I also want a list of those indicted people with the most to lose."

"OK." Thomas stood and stretched. "I'll drive in to Farmington and talk to a few of the people Freddie used to run with. There's a chance someone will know something we don't. The Indian underground is a whole other world."

"One thing more." Charlie paused, and cleared his throat. "Those people up there were just using Caleb for bait. I don't get the impression they intended us to ever actually have him. They may try to get him back."

Thomas frowned and nodded, then, with a backward glance at the baseball game, left for Farmington.

~~~~~~

Lucy Tallwoman and Sue Hanagarni laughed and talked as they watched six-year-old Caleb climbing through the tunnel maze at McDonalds.

"Looks like this is the first time he's ever been to one of these," Sue ventured. "He sure didn't want to take his shoes off." The boy stayed by himself, not interacting with the other children, but appeared to be enjoying himself nonetheless. There were several shopping bags of new clothes on the seats beside the women, and Sue exclaimed happily over the bargains they had found. "I wish I could find clothes to fit me this cheap!"

Lucy agreed. "It looks like he will at least have enough here to start school with this fall." She saw the look in Sue's eyes and went on, "Thomas and I had a talk. He asked me if I would go along with keeping the boy for good. That is if he can get legal custody of him." She toyed with the straw in her soda and looked up at Caleb, waving now from the top level of the play equipment. "I told him it would be good by me. I can't have any more kids. There's been something missing lately. Maybe this is it."

Sue looked away for a moment, waving at Caleb. "What about the girl?"

"Thomas said we would cross that bridge when we came to it. I think he has a bad feeling about the girl. We'll just have to wait and see."

"I've been thinking a lot about kids myself lately," Sue said, blushing slightly. "Charlie likes kids. He said he just hadn't realized it until he was around Caleb." She took a sip of her drink. "We've been talking too. I think he's about ready to make a...uh, you know, 'life change.' I found some real estate brochures on his desk the other day, and he keeps talking about getting a little place where he can have a horse or two." She smiled at Lucy. "Why would he need two horses?"

"It sounds to me like he's got a plan." Lucy was happy for Sue and hoped these indications meant what she thought they did.

The women left Lucy's father at the other end of the mall near the western-wear store, and Sue, looking at her watch, thought maybe they should head back that way. Lucy agreed and called to Caleb to come put his shoes on. As she gathered her purchases and adjusted her sunglasses, she noticed, out of the corner of her eye, a tall, dark man in a suit and tie. He was wearing mirrored sunglasses and watched intently as Caleb put his shoes on. The man had his long hair put up on the back of his neck in a bun, something you didn't see very often anymore. Occasionally, he would glance at the women's table. A chill fell across Lucy, and she still hadn't shaken it off as they left the restaurant.

They found Paul T'Sosi sitting on a bench by a little fountain with a pool and some goldfish. He had spent some time studying the fish and concluded there must be a good reason his people, traditionally, did not eat these creatures.

When the women walked up behind the bench, Paul jumped

when his daughter touched his shoulder. He could feel her hand trembling and looked around to see a shadow cross her face. She had Caleb by the hand, and the old man noticed her knuckles turning white. The boy was looking up at her with an odd expression but made no comment. The old man rose from the bench. He had wanted to take the boy into the western store to try on some boots but could see it would have to be another time.

"Time to go," Lucy urged, pulling at the boy and heading for the mall exit with a sharp backward glance.

Sue looked a little perplexed but fell in behind Lucy and the boy. The old man brought up the rear, furtively checking over his shoulder—for what, he did not know.

When they reached the truck, they said good-bye to Sue, and after loading up, Lucy Tallwoman stood a moment by the door, looking back at the mall exit. She saw nothing out of the ordinary, but again something cold passed over her, causing her to shiver. On the drive home she kept an eye on the rearview mirror and watched the side roads for strange vehicles. The old man, too, was watching from his place in the back seat of the truck. He leaned to the front to check the boy's seat belt. It was nice having this back seat in a truck, and he was beginning to see why most of their neighbors on the reservation had opted for this newer style. The clatter of the diesel engine did put him on edge at first, and he had told Thomas, "I believe there's something wrong with this damn thing! It sounds like it's ready to throw a rod all the time."

"No, Paul, that is just the way these engines are. They are very high compression and that makes them a little noisy." Thomas had become quite solicitous of the old man's feelings of late and tried to stay on his good side as much as possible.

Once home, the old man and the boy went down to the corrals to check on the sheep. Paul had thrown them some feed before they went to town but felt guilty they had not been taken out to pasture that day. He should have stayed home and done chores, but he had wanted to get the boy some proper boots. He wanted to see how the boy would do riding his old black mare.

~~~~~~

Hiram Buck was a very unhappy man. He had been paid for only two of the cows he had sold that morning at the sale. Payment had been withheld on a third due to some discrepancy the brand inspector found in the paperwork. He needed that money. He could explain the paperwork—he had done it before. He had even fixed brands before, but it would take time, and he was as short of time as he was money. The long and short of it was he was going to have to come up with another eight or nine hundred dollars pronto, and that was just for starters. He had finally come to the conclusion that he would have to sell his horse—the one he lent Charlie Yazzie the day before; the only horse he had left worth enough money to help. This put him in an evil mood. That horse was worth twice what it would bring at the sale barn. Today was the first of the month, and there would be a special horse auction following the livestock sale. It would not start until late afternoon, giving him time to go pick up the horse at his nephew's and check him into the sale.

The entire plan was becoming complicated. There were only two people in the whole family smart enough to pull this thing off—and one of them was dead.

What really grated on him was that his idiot nephew George Jim had botched a critical part of that plan. The money he'd counted on would not be forthcoming. Worse, it could lead to the loss of a much bigger amount of money further on. More money than he or anyone else in the family had ever seen at one time. Now, too, there was the matter of Sally's boy Caleb. He had high hopes for that boy. He was smart, and God knew there were few smart boys left in his bunch. In fact there were few boys at all. He was awash in girls—sullen, bad tempered girls.

He admitted he'd been a little rough on Caleb at first, but that was an uncle's job—to provide the structure and training fathers were too lax or soft to give, assuming the boy had any sort of real father to begin with. Hiram Buck had never met Thomas Begay, but he had heard plenty about him—all of it bad. Not the kind of bad he could live with either. It was the stupid kind of bad brought on by drinking and lack of self-respect. Hiram was not a drinker himself, but he had seen plenty of it. He was now the eldest and, by default, head of his family. It was no longer a "band" as it had once been, but it was all they had left, and he was in charge of it. There was no one coming up capable of taking his place as far as he could see.

~~~~~~~

Hiram drove up to his nephew's shabby, little trailer. George Jim was his dead wife's nephew. His wife Tilde and her sister had died within months of each other. The doctor said in both cases it was their heart, probably genetic. Both women were quite over-weight and of a querulous nature.

George Jim was a slow thinker but could usually be relied on to do what Hiram told him, and he was an excellent shot with a rifle. He was a rough-mannered, short-tempered boy who liked to fight, but today he looked like a whipped dog and would not look up as he opened the door for his uncle. Hiram pushed his way silently past him into the unkempt little trailer which had once belonged to George Jim's mother.

"Where's my horse?" he said softly. "You did at least pick up the horse, didn't you?"

These soft-spoken words of his uncle were a very bad sign. George Jim cringed inwardly.

The disastrous news of George Jim's failure had reached Hiram only hours before. The young niece who delivered the message was visibly shaken by the rage Hiram had flown into and on her return home stopped to warn George Jim.

He would not look at his uncle, but there was a spark of hope in his voice as he replied, "I got him alright. He's in the corral out back." He licked his lips and launched into it. "That sonofabitch horse of yours threw his head up just as I fired. By the time I worked my way off the rim and back around to my truck and trailer, that Navajo and the boy was already gone." He wished his Aunt Tilde were still alive. She was the only person who would ever stand up to Hiram. She had been a big woman, nearly as big as Hiram, and some said smarter, but just as mean natured. Not having any sons of her own, Tilde had doted on George Jim and had often run interference between him and Hiram. George searched now for something distracting to say. "You need to get some shoes on that horse. The quarters in the fronts are starting to break out, and he's got a crack in his off hind. He's going to cripple up on you if you don't work on those feet."

Hiram's eyes narrowed and he now spoke in a deadly whisper. "Don't you ever tell *me* how to do anything. You don't tell *me* what to do! I tell *you* what to do!" He backhanded his nephew, spinning George Jim halfway across the room and onto the floor. "A twelve year old could have done that job up in the canyon. You knew that horse would not pass the water without stopping. I told you that...and they would get off to let him drink. I set everything up for you. Even rolled the log out on the point so you would have cover and a rest to shoot from." Hiram was nearly shouting now, breathing hard and spitting his words through clinched teeth. "I spent all morning up there! Making sure everything was right. What! You only had one bullet? You couldn't take another shot?"

"I didn't want to hit the boy. You said to be careful of Caleb!" George Jim was still on the floor and had not even tried to get up. His right arm guarded his face and slobber was dribbling off his chin. He figured he was going to die right there in his mother's ratty, old trailer.

He started to say it was not his fault... But Hiram drew back a boot as though to kick him, then pointed a threatening finger. "Don't say another single word! I ought to kill you for this. But, I'm not. I'm going to give you one more chance—a chance to make things right, and then if you can't...then I'm going to kill you."

Hiram shook his head in disgust at his nephew and went slamming out of the trailer. He stood cursing in the yard for a moment then walked around back, briefly checked his horse over, and with a final expletive toward the house, loaded the horse and left for the sale barn.

George Jim pulled himself up onto the couch, waiting for the pounding in his ears to stop and thinking what a very lucky person he was to still be alive. A great wave of relief passed over him as he heard his uncle's truck pull out of the yard.

~~~~~~~

Later, Hiram Buck sat at his kitchen table and counted his money for the third time. The tickets from the stock sale were scattered near the brown grocery sack on which he was scribbling figures. Again and again with the stub of a pencil, he added the numbers together. He hoped somehow he was in error, that there might actually be more money than these figures allowed. He finally had to admit, however, that numbers do not lie. He was still hundreds of dollars short of his goal.

The woman at the bank would be disappointed. He sighed and crumpled the paper sack into a ball. He could feel everything slipping away. How could this relatively small amount of money determine the course of a man's life.

The fact was Hiram Buck had no friends left, not a single person he could call on, even for so small an amount of money as this. In olden times it was said of the *Ute*: "There is no term in their language for rich or poor in regard to material goods. A man who says he is rich means he has many friends; being poor means he has no friends." Hiram Buck was a very poor man indeed.

Hiram was contemplating an amount of money that could

change his family's life—not that he cared so much for the welfare of the family anymore. He thought there were few of them left who were worth the powder to blow them to hell. His nephew George Jim was a good example. Recently back from a tour of military duty, he had seen a good bit of action, acquitting himself as well as could be expected. The military conceded he was a very good shot with a rifle and a fine tracker, but that was about the extent of any God-given talent. When, finally, they couldn't figure out what else to do with him, he had been given a "Section Eight" discharge by army doctors. They had a more politically correct term for it now, but the meaning was the same. George Jim currently seemed content to just hang around his mother's old place, living on a small disability check. Hiram had given his sister-in-law that little piece of ground at the behest of his late wife; now he regretted it.

The original quarter section of land his grandfather left him was dwindling away—already relatives had wound up with over a fourth of it. True, they had paid Hiram for their small plots; nonetheless, at least they were family, and he did still wield considerable control as head of the clan. His grandfather had been one of the smartest men their band had ever produced, parlaying a small government land allotment into a rather admirable private holding—a holding he had thought might someday benefit his grandchildren. The old man, in his last years, had personally selected Hiram as his single heir, thinking he, like himself, would continue to look out for the family.

Hiram liked to believe he had the family's best interest at heart, but it had become complicated these last few years, and now, with Tilde gone, his heart was no longer in it.

This bank foreclosure thing was something he did not fully understand. Tilde had always taken care of these things; it had not been his job! What he had finally been made to understand by the loan officer was that the grace period on his long-overdue loan payments had ended some time ago. Without the arrears being paid in full by next Thursday morning, the sheriff would be notified to serve an eviction notice on his remaining parcel of land. Hiram had begun saving for this eventuality when the notices first started appearing in his rural mailbox. He had placed them all in a little package in his closet, but he never looked at them and had only opened the first one or two. Over the past months he had sold off nearly everything of value, including the last of the cows, one of which was not even his. That cow was now in brand inspection hell, and any help it might provide would come too late in his estimation. The problem was his grandfather had placed the land in a family trust. None of it could ever be sold, except to a blood relative. What had been meant to preserve the land for the family now insured its loss. The one possible salvation was his niece Sally Klee.

The people who had come to Sally Klee in secret, trying to buy her silence in the Greyhorse case, had let it be known they would pay good money for the silence of other prosecution witnesses as well. While they thought Thomas Begay might be approachable in this regard, they had been advised Charlie Yazzie would not. "Something would have to be done about Charlie Yazzie," they said.

Sally Klee had at first been disinclined to take advantage of this dubious windfall, thinking it something beyond her ability to deal with, at least on her own. She had been back for several months and could now see she had little future with her *Ute* cousins. In a moment of panic, she felt she had no other choice but to go to her Uncle Hiram and tell him of the offer to buy her silence.

It did not take Hiram Buck long to convince her that it was indeed a golden opportunity and certainly in her and the children's best interest, not to mention a chance to repay her adoptive clan for their generous support over the years. Hiram felt so strongly in this regard he immediately moved Sally's son and daughter to separate families among the relatives for safekeeping. He told Sally it was for their own good. It would shield them from harm, he said.

He later took charge of the negotiations himself and assured those people he could take care of Charlie Yazzie and Thomas Begay as well should Thomas prove to be a problem money couldn't fix.

Sally now grew beside herself with worry for her children and felt she made a serious mistake in going to Hiram. She was terrified at what might happen should she not fall in with Hiram's plan. It had never occurred to her he would involve her children. She had grown up watching his manipulation of other family members and knew what he was capable of when crossed. Sally Klee did not consider herself a smart person, but she did have her people's instinct for survival. She well understood that desperate people must sometimes do desperate things.

3

The Horse

Thomas fiddled with the air conditioner as Charlie's new government-issue truck ticked off the miles to Cortez. "This air is really nice. Not quite hot enough for it yet, but it's nice to know you have it when you need it."

Charlie glanced over at him and raised an eyebrow. "That Dodge you bought has air, doesn't it?"

"Well, yeah, but you have to rev that diesel up quite a bit before the compressor kicks in. Just idling around town it sort of dies away. It seemed to work okay when we bought it this spring."

Charlie nodded. "Isn't that always the way?"

"Yep, that's how it goes. First your money, then the hose." Thomas had picked up a lot of these little sayings back when he was drinking and still liked to work them into the conversation from time to time.

What Thomas didn't like was the idea of poking around up there in *Ute* country. The *Ute* were a curious people, at least those related to Sally Klee were. In past times they were nomads, roaming their huge homeland with only what they could carry on their backs—unlike the *Dinè* who built permanent *hogans* and did a little rudimentary farming. He knew it rankled the *Ute* that they'd once controlled one of the largest areas of the Rocky Mountains and now had to be satisfied with much less. The Navajo, on the other hand, were a fairly sedentary people, living, for the most part, in small family groups. Yet, the Navajo Nation consisted of more than 25,000 square miles, including vast coal and even some timber reserves—the largest Indian reservation in the world. Admittedly, most of that land was sand and rock, but even those portions might have oil and gas reserves. The *Dinè* felt quite fortunate whites had been unaware of those mineral reserves when they had finally ceded this land to them.

Charlie wasn't sure yet how he was going to handle this matter with Hiram Buck. He had no proof of wrongdoing at this point. He thought the key might lie in finding Sally Klee and her daughter. He suspected Sally would not be easy to find.

Charlie's search of related Legal Services case files also produced no useful information, and calls to various chapter houses came up empty too. Sally's last known address (never verified) now came up listed as unknown. Thomas had not come across anything of use in Farmington either. It was now in the back of his mind that something bad might have already happened to Sally and possibly his daughter as well. There was a hard, cold thing in the pit of his stomach when he let himself think of it.

There wasn't much traffic on an early Sunday morning approaching Cortez, and purely on a hunch, Charlie decided to stop by the sale barn to see if they had a ticket documenting the sale of Hiram Buck's cows. If, indeed, he actually sold any cows, his address should be on the ticket.

Though it was Sunday, the business office was open, along with the cafe and loading docks. Saturday night horse sales ran late into the evening, and many buyers chose to pick up their animals Sunday morning.

As they parked the truck in the crowded lot, Thomas looked around at the still-full corrals and whistled. "It must have been quite a sale!" He climbed down from the truck and ambled over to the holding pens, Charlie not far behind. "I need to get me another horse," he declared. "That mare of the old man's is getting a little long in the tooth for any serious work." Thomas knew horses and learned how to ride about the same time he learned how to walk, as did most Navajo boys. Even Charlie had learned to ride at an early age, though he had grown a bit rusty in his time away from the reservation. Charlie's father had been a well-known contender at the local rodeos, and his grandfather bred good horses according to those who remembered him.

As they leaned on the fence rail, Charlie mentioned how much he had liked that horse of Hiram Buck's. "I really don't have a place to keep a horse right now…I'm just sort of thinking ahead. If we get us a little place, I wouldn't mind having a couple."

Thomas noted the "us" and "couple" and smiled to himself. "Well, you know you can always keep horses out at our place." He thought it would be good to have more than one horse about. Horses do better when there is more than one.

"I'll think about that," Charlie said as they left the corrals and made their way through the parking lot back to the business office.

A tough-looking white woman with large tortoise-shell glasses was in charge of several younger girls wading through the paperwork the state required in a livestock sale. A double line formed at the counter—one for buyers, another for sellers. The boss woman stood behind the girls, arms folded across an ample bosom, alert to the slightest error. Charlie pushed forward between the lines and flashed his gold badge at the woman, who put on her mean face and motioned him to a clear spot at the end. She put her hands on the counter and leaned forward menacingly. "How can we help you?" She was clearly annoyed and in no mood to waste time on Charlie.

Charlie held her gaze and kept the badge in her face. "We need some information regarding a sale you may have made yesterday."

Thomas was somewhat taken aback at Charlie's attitude with this authority figure. Other Indians, waiting their turn, smiled and nudged one another as the woman hesitated, finally stepping back and dropping her hands. "What's the name?" she asked.

Charlie put the badge away. "Hiram Buck."

"Buyer or seller?"

"Seller."

The woman reached over and took a sheaf of papers from the girl in charge of those transactions and expertly leafed through them. "Hiram Buck...three cows. One of them a no-sale due to a hold by the brand inspector." She looked up at Charlie for a moment. "Is this about that brand inspection?"

"Possibly. I need an address on him."

The woman wrote down the address on a pad, tore it off, and passed it to Charlie, who thanked her and turned to go.

"Just a minute!" the woman called after him. "There's another ticket here. He brought in a horse later in the afternoon for the evening sale."

Charlie turned. "What kind of horse?"

"Eight-year-old sorrel gelding. It hasn't been picked up yet. Pen 104, if you need to look at it." She jerked a thumb over her shoulder at the clock and lowered her eyes. "We're only in the office till noon."

Again, Charlie thanked the woman, who sniffed and thrust the tickets back to a helper to straighten out. She shook her head, watching Charlie and Thomas through the front window as they walked toward the government truck.

Halfway to the Chevy, Charlie paused, looking thoughtful. "Let's go look at that horse."

Thomas, still slightly awed by the way Charlie had bulldozed the office manager, fell into line behind him without a word. Charlie was getting to be quite the smart-ass Indian, he thought proudly. Pen 104 was down a series of alleyways. Most of the stock in that section had already been picked up. The horse had its head over the gate, and Charlie recognized him immediately even before they reached the pen. He opened the gate and held his hand out for the gelding to snuffle on. Thomas came in behind him and looked the horse over with a critical eye. Charlie talked to it in a low voice and rubbed its jaw, which he thought had a calming effect. The horse spent the morning tossing his head and trotting around the pen, calling anxiously to the others as they were led off by their new owners. This gelding had not been to town much and was out of his element.

"This is the horse Hiram Buck lent me to go get Caleb," Charlie said. "I had a hunch it might be. I'm surprised he would let him go at auction. It's a better horse than that." Charlie felt a growing affinity for this gelding. He still thought it may have saved his life back up there in the canyon.

Thomas ran his hand down the horse's off hind leg, picking up the foot and examining a crack in the hoof wall. "This crack's going to get worse if it don't get trimmed up and shod. He's overdue by a good bit." He shook his head. "I'm surprised Hiram had him up in that rough country with his feet in this shape."

"They probably weren't in this shape when he took him up there. This horse had some miles put on him up there."

Thomas stepped back to look at the horse. "Not a bad put-together old boy...for a using horse. I wonder who bought him last night?"

"I think we're about to find out," Charlie said with a push of his chin up the alleyway.

An older, thin-lipped white woman in a cowboy hat and faded Levi jacket was coming up the alleyway with a halter slung over her shoulder and an inquiring look on her face. This woman obviously spent a lot of her life out in the sun, and Charlie couldn't put a number on her age.

"Howdy," she called, "how do you boys like my new horse?" She was not quite smiling when she said this but appeared to be of a good humor.

Charlie stepped forward and stuck out his hand. "My friend and

I like him just fine. We were just saying it's a shame he has that cracked hoof." He threw a sad look at the foot as he said this.

Thomas smiled to himself and turned back to the horse. Charlie meant to buy this horse if he could. Thomas was no stranger to horse trading, and he could read where this was going.

Charlie's grandmother had been quite a horse trader herself after his grandfather had passed away. She was Charlie's sole support and had not been afraid to step into the family business. Charlie learned a lot about horses and horse trading by the time he left for college. His grandmother insisted he go, however, telling him, "There is no future in horse trading anymore." Well, he wanted this horse, and here it had nearly fallen into his lap. Someone or something was looking out for him.

The woman in the hat nodded at his name and shook hands. "Aida Winters. I must be getting old," she grinned. "I'd have caught that foot back in the day. Easy fix though—a set of shoes and a little pine tar will set him right pretty quick, I imagine."

"Damn," Thomas thought to himself. "A woman horse trader!" Women often made shrewd traders and drove hard bargains. He himself preferred not to deal with them.

The woman looked them both up and down. "You boys wouldn't be interested in him, would you? I got plenty of damn horses already; don't know why I put my hand up on this one. Just seemed like a good pony for the money, I reckon." She lowered her eyes demurely. "I dabble in stock from time to time, though lord knows I usually come out on the short end of the stick." As she talked she moved to the horse and with a little pinch behind his ears caused him to drop his nose into the rope halter she was holding. She brought the tag end smoothly around the top of his poll, securing it in a neat knot behind his left ear.

Charlie nodded but secretly doubted this woman ever lost much money on a horse. "We like him alright, if the price works for us." He shook his head. "I shouldn't even be looking at horses today.

I'm up here on other business."

"You in the law business? I saw you flashing a badge at that old hide in the office." She was grinning outright now, looking at him with what might have been a glimmer of respect.

He passed her a card and nodded, opening the gate as they talked. The two men walked along with her as she led the horse to the checkout station. She twirled the short end of the lead rope as she walked to keep the horse's mind on his business. "There's a farrier up there at the cafe having lunch; he owes me a favor. I'll see if he can throw a set of shoes on this pony while I buy you boys a burger." She paused and winked. "I'll write it off as a business expense."

She passed the horse by the gate attendant, who barely looked at her receipt. She was, apparently, well known there. They crossed the parking lot to her stock trailer and tied the horse alongside several others with auction tags still glued to their rumps. She turned toward Charlie. "I heard you asking about Hiram Buck over in the office. He must have been in bad need of money yesterday. I've tried to buy this horse off him before, but he wouldn't even talk about it."

Charlie missed a step. "You know Hiram Buck?"

"Everyone hereabouts knows Hiram. I live not far from him...as the crow flies." She frowned. "We've had dealings in the past. He's not going to be happy with me getting this horse, and cheap at that."

Thomas now interrupted by clearing his throat. He had been admiring her string of horses and spoke for the first time. "It looks like you made quite a haul last night." He knew from the quality of these animals that Aida Winters knew her business and wasn't one to trifle with in a trade.

"Yep, this dry spring is making for a lot of bargains. People can't afford hay anymore." She went to the tack compartment at the front of the trailer, opening it to display five or six used saddles and a pile of bridles and other tack. "I could suit you boys out to-day at prices you would be hard pressed find anywhere else…assuming, of course, you're in the market."

Thomas hung back, admiring a big piebald gelding with a glint in his eye. He liked a lot of "spirit" in a horse, and this one looked like he might serve that up on a daily basis.

Aida did not fail to notice Thomas's interest in the horse and called back to him, "That one's a bit salty yet. He might not suit you."

Thomas just smiled.

In the restaurant, Aida went to talk to the horseshoer while the two men found a table against the back wall and began studying the menu. Charlie leaned over and asked Thomas, "What do you think that sorrel horse is worth…not that I have any business buying him of course." He wondered what Sue would think about him messing around with horse deals when they were supposed to be looking for Sally Klee and Thomas's daughter. He could see Thomas had been thinking the same thing.

Thomas put his menu down. "You know, this woman might be exactly who we're looking for in the way of information about Hiram Buck. I don't have any problem mixing business with business." He glanced over at Aida. "I don't know how much that sorrel horse you want is worth, but I do know that woman will skin us like a couple of ground squirrels if we're not careful." He looked up at the ceiling a moment. "I'm going to say he's worth about twelve hundred dollars, but I doubt she has more than eight in him, including the shoeing." He squinted his eyes. "Nine hundred ought to buy him—he hasn't even left the sale yard yet, for God's sake.

Charlie agreed. "I'm thinking a couple of saddle horses might come in handy up here. For one thing I would like to take a look at that place where I got shot at." He rubbed his chin. "No telling where this thing is going to lead us."

"Whoa!" Thomas exclaimed. "I've only got fifty dollars on me.

I doubt Aida Winters does any horse financing for such as me."

Charlie looked thoughtfully over at Aida, who was still deep in conversation with the farrier. "You might be surprised," was all he said.

Aida got back to the table at about the same time the waitress made an appearance. Business was brisk and the woman was sweating. Blowing a wisp of straggly brown hair from her eyes, she looked at the unlikely trio. "What'll it be, folks? We've got the chili cheeseburger on special, and that comes with fries and a drink." She looked at the two Navajos. "We got fresh cherry lime-ade too, but its twenty-five cents extra on account of us using real limes instead of that phony bottled crap."

After they ordered, Aida mentioned the farrier was going to get right on the sorrel gelding. She figured he could have him done by the time they finished lunch. "See," she assured them, "just as easy as that!" She looked from one to the other and continued, "Now what do I have to do to fix you boys up with those horses? I'm already throwing in a free set of shoes." She turned to Thomas, raising a finger as she saw he was about to say something. "That piebald already has a good set of shoes on him!" Thomas had been about to ask if she would throw in a bridle but now thought better of it.

Charlie hesitated only a moment before deciding to lay it all out for her. "We are up here looking for Thomas's daughter and her mother Sally Klee," indicating Thomas with his chin. "Hiram Buck is related to them and might know where they are, though he's not apt to tell us anything. There must be other people who know as well. We are just going to have to ferret them out, one way or the other." Here he rubbed his forehead as though pondering what next to say. "We might be interested in those horses if the price was right." He paused. "And some saddles too, but first we need to find a place to camp for a few days while we check things out." He said this while looking directly at Aida. Thomas was appalled at so direct a ploy and looked away.

Aida, for her part, was not much taken aback but rather appeared surprisingly interested in their plight. Her eyes were sympathetic as she made her proposal. "I'll let you boys have those horses for not much more than I gave for them."

"Honest Injun?" Thomas asked with a grin.

Aida chuckled. "I don't have any feed in them yet and very little else. I want nine hundred for that sorrel. Six fifty for the other. Not just anyone will be able to ride that piebald," she cautioned. "Not for very long anyway." She hesitated and then went on, "You can pick out a couple of saddles to use while you're up here and decide later if they suit you enough to take home. If I can't trust the law, who can I trust?"

Charlie was always amazed at the power of a badge and a business card. He didn't even have jurisdiction off the reservation.

She frowned suddenly, remembering their mention of Hiram Buck. "There's no love lost between me and the Buck clan. I grew up here and have lived across the valley from them most of my life. You will want to be very careful dealing with Hiram Buck. His wife passed away a while back. That would have mellowed most men, but it just made Hiram meaner."

Charlie nodded and then looked over at Thomas, raising a questioning eyebrow. Thomas nodded assent, and the deal was struck for the horses. Charlie had his checkbook in the truck. This was going to take a good chunk out of the down payment he was saving for that little place in the country.

The brand inspector was still on the grounds, fortunately, and reissued bills of sale with only a little grumbling about private horse deals in the parking lot. This after-sale horse swapping was wearing him down; his feet were tired and he wanted to go home. As he walked away he called back, "Aida! If you see Hiram Buck, you tell him there's a cow up here he's going to owe a feed bill on if he can't explain how he got her."

Aida nodded to him and then turned to the boys. "Hiram brings some cows down from his relations on the Uinta Reserve now and again." She looked off into the distance. "The paperwork's always a mess." She pointed after the brand inspector. "Dan always has a time with those brands. Hiram's relatives up there are a pretty wild bunch from what I've heard. They all had the same great-grandpa as the Bucks, I guess." She smiled. "The nuts don't fall far from the tree, I expect."

She told the boys they could turn their horses loose in her corral and maybe camp out in her barn for a few days should they be of a mind. Charlie concluded this woman was a straight shooter and could be trusted. Thomas did not know what to think but was ready to do whatever it might take to find his daughter.

~~~~~~

Later that afternoon at Aida Winters' place, Charlie and Thomas pitched in to help put her new horses out to pasture. She thanked them, though they knew she could just as easily have managed by herself. Thomas offered to buy a couple of bales of hay to see them through their stay, but she waved him off saying, "If you boys could just restack them loose and leaning bales, that will be payment enough." Before taking her leave, she mentioned that Hiram Buck's place was just across the back pastures. "If you keep to that timbered ridge running along the north side, you can't miss it." She went on to say her place bordered one corner of the Buck property, and the precise property line, among other things, had always been a bone of contention. With a glance at the lowering skies and a quick wave, she made her way to the house and was not seen again that night.

Charlie and Thomas stacked their gear in one of the stalls and ate a cold dinner out of cans. Thomas said he would just as soon spread his blankets outside to sleep, but Charlie thought it might rain and felt it best they take advantage of the comforts of this barn while they could. It really didn't matter to Thomas; he could sleep anywhere. After restacking the hay they stood at the open barn door catching their breath and looking out across the land.

This seemed a fine country to the two *Dinè*. Wooded draws coursed through high meadows, sprinkled with ground-watered swales, gradually falling away to the dark canyons of federal land. The people in this country raised pinto beans and the hard, red winter wheat so favored by the Mormons. They were dry-land farmers, for the most part. The area had become quite famous for its beans. The land was well suited for it. The *Anasazi* farmed corn and beans here for more than a thousand years. The ruins of their ceaseless building dotted the countryside in profusion, causing modern farmers to plow around them to avoid the buried rock walls. Nearly every bean field had a sagebrush-covered mound, hiding what used to be a thriving little complex. It was generally thought the population was actually greater in those times than it was now.

The men turned their horses loose in the corral and stood watching them. After only a minute or two of fidgeting, Thomas grabbed a saddle and bridle and went into the corral to get acquainted with the piebald gelding. "I expect I might be better off trying this horse out now than in the morning when he's fresh."

Charlie, feeling himself well enough acquainted with his own horse, watched amused as Thomas's efforts to catch the piebald stirred up the dust. "You want some help?"

"Nahhh, I'll get him!" The gelding knew some tricks, but so did Thomas, who soon had the halter and lead rope back on him, snubbing him up short to the post set in the center of the corral. "He's a little ouchy from that trailer ride...just has to get his mind right." He whistled to the horse to keep his attention. "These snubbing posts are a handy thing to have." In his opinion, tying a green horse to a fence rail had caused some serious horse wrecks.

The piebald stood fairly still while Thomas shook out a saddle blanket around his head and flopped it back and forth across his withers and then flanks. Charlie came over to help him get the saddle on, but it really wasn't necessary. The two were almost disappointed in just how easy it all was. Thomas put his weight in the near stirrup a couple of times before climbing aboard and setting his feet deep in the stirrups. He was confident in his ability to ride this horse and did not feel the need to edge into it. Charlie released the bull snap on the lead rope. The horse knew instantly he was free and gathered himself for a mighty leap—straight up. He nearly swapped ends at the top of the jump and came down with a bone-jarring crash, nearly unseating Thomas, who was lucky to grab the horn on the way up. The horse stood there a moment, head down, legs splayed, and then calmly shook himself, straightened up, and walked off, head high, as though such a display was quite ordinary and to be expected.

Charlie slapped his leg and laughed. "Do you suppose he does that every time?"

"I hope not. I'm a little out of practice these days." Thomas managed through clinched teeth, "I just think he was testing me." Reaching down and patting the horse's neck, he added, "I hope I passed." Thomas himself was grinning now and proceeded to put the horse through a few basic rollbacks and figure eights before pulling him up short in front of Charlie. "Acts like he remembers a thing or two. He just forgot his manners for a minute, is all."

Charlie could see he was pleased with the horse despite the rough start.

Thomas did like the horse and thought Charlie's money well spent. "I'll get you the cash when we get back home," he said half seriously from atop the horse as though not paying him back had ever been an option.

"That's good," Charlie grinned. "I'd hate to have to beat it out of you."

It was almost dark, but Thomas had Charlie open the gate and took the gelding for a lope around the pasture, bringing him back breathing hard and sweating around the eyes. "This horse will do," he smiled. "At least people won't be borrowing him all the time."

Up at the house Sally Klee peered out from the edge of the living room curtains. "I see Thomas can still ride," she told the woman at her shoulder. "Not as good as when he was drinking though." Aida Winters nodded but said nothing.

~~~~~~~~

Aida Winters had long been of the opinion the Buck clan had no redeeming qualities whatsoever. Most of them, she thought, didn't have enough sense to pour piss out of a boot, and as a whole, she had seldom encountered a more ill-natured and deceitful family. The one exception was Hiram's niece Sally Klee, and she was neither a full-blooded family member or, for that matter, a full-blooded *Ute*.

Sally, when she was still small, would find her way down to Aida's place every chance she got, spending time helping Aida with little chores (weeding the garden and such) before her mother would come storming down to take her home. This had been just after Aida's husband died. She was lonely then and needed something to occupy her time. She became quite fond of the girl, sometimes helping her with her schoolwork and correcting her English when she could. Sally had been caught up in the confusion of learning three languages at the same time. Her mother spoke good Navajo and insisted on using the language to communicate with her daughter when she didn't want the Buck clan to know what was being said. Sally's English never really became what Aida thought it should be.

Aida recently heard Sally was back up at the Buck place, and with two small children too. So it was not a complete surprise when, late one evening well after dark, she heard a timorous knock at her back door. It was Sally Klee, and it was immediately apparent she was in some distress, nearly out of breath and trembling.

She stood there looking at Aida, tears welling up in her eyes, wringing her hands, shoulders shaking. Aida opened the screen door and pulled her gently inside. She knew some grave misfortune had befallen the girl and led her to the kitchen table where she nearly had to help her into a chair. After putting on the teakettle, she turned back to Sally, who was wiping her eyes on her sleeves and whimpering to herself like a puppy. Aida set cups and spoons on the table and went back to preparing the tea. Sally, unlike most Indians, had always been fond of tea, probably learned from Aida. In Aida's experience it seemed most Indians preferred the more robust flavor of coffee.

As she filled their cups, Aida spoke soothingly to the girl as she once had spoken to her as a child. "What's happened up there…Hiram didn't hurt you, did he?" There had been many rumors over the years, and Aida would put nothing past Hiram Buck.

The girl had not heard a kindly word spoken in a long time, and the tears flowed in earnest now as she reached out for Aida's hand. "They have my kids!" she cried almost incoherently. "They won't give them back…Caleb and Ida are gone" Her voice trailed off in heartrending sobs.

Those bastards! Aida thought. What have they done now? "Tell me Sally," she said gripping her hand more firmly, "why did they take your children?"

The girl's sad eyes ranged around the old familiar kitchen. "Hiram has gotten in with some very bad people and talked me into going along with them too. It's a bad thing they want me to do, and they are keeping the kids until it's done." Slowly she began to tell Aida her story, not leaving anything out, causing Aida's throat to tighten and her own eyes to fill by the time she was finished.

"Drink your tea, sweetheart," she said finally. "Give me a little time to think." She now sipped her own tea in a silent rage.

Sally had been at Aida Winters only two days when Aida returned from the livestock auction followed by a strange pickup truck. She stared from behind the bedroom curtains in amazement as Thomas and Charlie got out and started unloading horses.

Sally had not seen Thomas since the afternoon nearly six months ago when he and Charlie Yazzie had come to her place looking for Freddy Chee. They said he might be involved in the

Patsy Greyhorse murder, and what would turn out to be one of the more notorious corruption cases in tribal memory. She knew Freddy later tried to drag Thomas Begay down with him, but thanks to Charlie Yazzie, Thomas eventually was exonerated. It was said the experience had a life-altering effect on Thomas, bringing about changes most people previously thought impossible.

4

The Marksman

Charlie and Thomas saddled up early the next morning. While the piebald gelding pranced and snorted, he didn't offer another aerial display. They were nearly halfway along the ridge to the Buck place when Charlie thought about the revolver he had left in the glove box of the truck. He didn't mention it to Thomas, who he knew would not be pleased at the news. Thomas set great store by that pistol, calling it their "good luck piece."

Charlie's relatives, who had presented him the gun at the start of his career, never tired of hearing how it had once saved the men's lives. They liked the story best when told by Thomas, who embellished it in a fashion that both embarrassed Charlie and strengthened his resolve not to count too much on his shooting skills in the future. He felt he was generally better off without the gun. Without some specific reason, he seldom even thought to carry it anymore. He almost never practiced with it and hoped he would not have to stake his life on it again.

Thomas Begay, when he and Sally lived together, had only once gone with her to visit the Bucks, and he now hardly remembered any of the clan he had met. George Jim had been in the service at the time, and Sally's mother had passed away years before. His strongest memory was of Tilde Buck. She had thought Sally and her nephew George Jim might hit it off eventually when he returned from the service. She had not been prepared to like Thomas, though he had been on his best behavior and did not drink during their short stay. Hiram Buck had been absent, up north pursuing the purchase of some stock from a distant relative on the Uintah

Reservation. Thomas spent most of his time poking around the countryside by himself. It was Mormon country and hard to find a drink if you didn't know the right people.

They tied their horses in a small copse of trees and eased up on-to the Buck property in the shelter of a slight draw angling off the ridge. It was not hard to tell when they hit Hiram's land—the grass immediately disappeared and there were signs of severe overgrazing, even though no cows were to be seen. Crossing Aida's fence was like coming into a different sort of country altogether.

Thomas looked around. "This place has gone way downhill from what I remember." He kicked a dried cow pie. "Hiram and his bunch must have fallen on hard times to let the place get in this condition."

Charlie nodded agreement. "I can see where these people might be open to an opportunity to make a little extra cash."

Thomas again thought back to the visit he and Sally once made in which her Aunt Tilde talked incessantly about her sister's son, George Jim, and the fine little place he had not far from her and Hiram's. She thought the boy would do well when his time in the service was up. She kept a picture of him on the wall and kept bringing it to Sally's attention, hoping Thomas would get the idea. The picture showed a dark, broad-faced young man with small eyes and bushy hair. He was wearing military fatigues, which somehow suited him. Hiram's picture hung right next to it, and while Thomas had seen the family resemblance, the boy had appeared weak beside Hiram.

The morning was warming up, and they stopped for a break and drink of water when, far in the distance, gunshots attracted their attention. They sounded too far off to pose any immediate concern, and the two men just looked at one another.

Thomas counted the shots, holding up a hand and enumerating the evenly spaced rounds finger by finger. "Five shots. That's a full magazine for a hunting rifle."

Charlie nodded. "Sounds like target practice to me." He had no more than said this when another five shots punctuated the morning calm.

"Yep, someone, at least, is out to sharpen his eye." Thomas said this with the sad shake of his head he used when speaking of Charlie's marksmanship.

Remaining concealed, they worked their way out to the end of the draw. They could see across a considerable meadow, or what had once been a meadow in better days. On a barren rise an old trailer house stood watch over the remains of a few rusted trucks and scattered trash of daily living. A man was resting a rifle across the hood of a pickup truck, taking aim at a very distant target. From what they could see, the target was remarkably small. Still, even at this distance the two could see little puffs of dust from exactly behind the target. The man could shoot, that was certain.

Thomas looked at Charlie from where they knelt, sheltered in a small declivity. "I wonder if that's your shooter?"

"Well, if it is I'm surprised he missed me. One thing's for sure: he would make a likely recruit for anyone in the market for such talent."

They noticed the man carefully picking up his spent brass from the hood after each volley.

"I don't think you'll find any shell casing up there in the canyon where you were shot at." Thomas rubbed his chin. "Probably a reloader, too…most of these sharpshooters are."

They decided this might not be the best time to have this person discover them watching and quietly withdrew the way they had come. Thomas remembered the trailer once belonged to Tilde's sister. It appeared this man doing the shooting lived there alone. No sign of a woman was to be seen. Thomas felt sure the shooter was George Jim.

"I don't think we will find Sally there," Thomas ventured.

As they made their way back to the horses, Thomas seemed deep in thought and finally wondered aloud, "How do you suppose they knew you would be having lunch in that cafe up in Bluff? You know…so Hiram could lure you up the canyon looking for Caleb?"

Charlie pondered the question. "I've given that a lot of thought. I don't think they did know. I think I was followed there from my phony appointment in Blanding. I believe Hiram would have eventually pulled me over with his little story regardless. I think the cafe was a lucky opportunity more than anything else." He paused to wipe his forehead. "The real question is how I got called out to

Blanding in the first place. I looked at the case file when I got back, and it was an actual case, but the woman involved never left the reservation, according to the records."

"So how do you explain Hiram's niece working in the cafe?" asked Thomas, not willing to let it go.

"Now, that may have been a coincidence," Charlie admitted uncertainly. He held up a finger. "As long as we are on the subject of unlikely events, how did Sally Klee come to be living in Farmington with you and Freddy? She was raised right here, wasn't she?"

Thomas told the story as simply as he could. "Well, about the time Sally turned eighteen, an old aunt on her Navajo side had to go to a government care facility and sent word Sally could have her *hogan* near Farmington. Sally's half-brother Freddy Chee, who brought the message, offered to take her back down to Farmington with him. She jumped at the chance." Thomas went on a bit sadly, "Sally thought this would be a good move. I guess she thought she would find a happier life there." He went on to tell how the Buck clan, with its sullen, ill-tempered girls, attracted few young men of a caliber suited for husbands. He thought Sally might have been afraid she would end up like her cousins. Thomas did not like to think about those times and withdrew from the conversation. They rode the rest of the way back to Aida's in complete silence, though there was much more he could have said.

The fact of the business was that Freddy Chee had ulterior motives for taking his half-sister to Farmington. He had been on his own since he was sixteen and was quite worldly in Sally's view. Still, he had sunk to lows she could not fathom. Once settled near the more cosmopolitan Farmington, it had not taken her long to become enamored of Freddy's good-looking friend Thomas Begay. She thought Thomas bright, quick-witted, and funny. In short, all the things she had found lacking at the Bucks. Thomas had a good job working as a mechanic in the tribal shops and could be very entertaining when sober. The couple immediately took up housekeeping in what now was considered Sally's *hogan*. Freddy Chee was somewhat displeased with the arrangement but had a life of his own, and there were many other prospects to sidetrack his attention.

The young couple spent a good portion of their spare time hanging around the Indian bars in the back section of Farmington and became well known among that element. Sally even took up drinking, herself, for a while until she became pregnant and realized where that path led. All in all, and having little better to compare it with, Sally thought her life in that new place a fairly happy one. It was only after the children came that Thomas's drinking worsened, finally to the point he was unable to function in any sensible way. He soon lost his good job, causing him to depend on odd jobs working on cars that belonged to people who did not always pay.

Sally, more and more, had to depend on handouts from Freddy Chee in order to keep the little family going. It was then that Freddy had returned and ordered Thomas out, not having had it in mind to support his sister when he brought her down there—quite the contrary in fact. Freddy had his finger in many pies.

It was late afternoon when Charlie and Thomas finally arrived back at Aida's barn. As they pulled the saddles off their horses, Charlie looked toward the house but saw no sign of anyone stirring.

~~~~~~~

That night, after the light in the barn had gone out, Aida told Sally that, from what she had gathered in conversation with Thomas and Charlie, Caleb was now in a safe place. She did not know how they had come by the boy. She only knew the two were now determined to find Sally and Ida.

While Sally was greatly relieved at this news of her son and grateful for Thomas stepping in, she was still desperately worried about her daughter and what might happen should he interfere with Hiram's plans. Both women agreed it might be best if no one knew Sally's whereabouts. The less anyone knew about that, they thought, the better.

~~~~~~~

Sue Hanagarni thought Pete Fish had been acting rather strangely the last few days. He seemed particularly upset to see Charlie's name penciled in on the callboard as on vacation.

"When did Charlie Yazzie put in for vacation time?" he asked, looking confused. "I didn't see that come across my desk." Not that Charlie being out of the way bothered him. It gave him more of a free hand with Sue. But it did bother him not knowing what he was up to. Charlie Yazzie had become a serious thorn in the side of many important people of late, and his recent rise in the "old man's" favor worried Pete Fish.

Sue had an answer ready for that one. "Pete, Charlie put in for those days months ago." She laughed. This was not strictly true of course, but Sue's allegiance lay with Charlie. "You didn't forget again, did you?" The office staff loved teasing Pete Fish about his poor memory, even though it was apparent he took the taunts seriously, and as office manager often retaliated in secret little paybacks. He was never an easygoing administrator, and after the corruption shakeup, had become nearly paranoid—seemed to have it in for nearly everyone in the office, except Sue, of course. He was as cloyingly attentive to her as ever. It was becoming an embarrassment, but he seemed not to notice. She had never given Pete Fish the slightest encouragement. Nonetheless, he had lately done everything possible to extend his brief office encounters with her and now seemed more determined than ever to have a relationship with the younger woman. The flowers on her desk every Monday morning were beginning to get on her nerves. Not that she didn't like flowers. She just wished Charlie would send a few now and then.

She thought Charlie's reaction a bit odd when she told him it was Pete Fish who requested he travel up north for a deposition—a deposition Charlie thought could just as easily been handled by tribal police. She was beginning to think Charlie was keeping something to himself, or maybe he was just going through one of his little bouts of jealousy. If he was so jealous why didn't he get off the dime and do something about it. An engagement ring would be nice, and it might make Pete Fish go away, too. There had been some encouraging signs of late, and Charlie seemed to be inching in the right direction, but she would be an old lady before he made his move at this rate.

It was nearly quitting time when Lucy Tallwoman dropped by the office and asked Sue if they could talk.

"Sure, let's drop by the Dinè Bikeyah for a cup of coffee."

After the women had settled themselves in a booth and ordered, Lucy nervously looked around the nearly full cafe. "I know you're going to think I'm crazy, but I'm pretty sure someone is after Caleb."

"Is that what that fast exit at the mall was all about Sunday?" Sue stirred her coffee. "I didn't see anything unusual…but then I'm not the most observant person in the world either."

Lucy nodded. "And I might not have seen anything that really meant anything either, but Thomas told me before he left with Charlie that he had reason to believe someone might try to get Caleb back." She frowned. "I don't know whether he meant Caleb's mother or what." She darted a glance at the parking lot where the after-work dinner crowd was beginning to sift in, oilfield hands mostly, guys living in motels with no place else to go. A black Suburban with tinted windows pulled up in front, paused a moment as though judging how busy the place was, and then drove off in the direction of town.

"Well, I'm not surprised you're on edge if Thomas said that. Who wouldn't be? What the hell's wrong with him anyway, saying that and then taking off, leaving you alone here." That wasn't quite true of course. Lucy had her father, but still it did seem she was pretty much up against it by herself.

"Yeah, that's probably it alright. I've just got it in my head that something's going to happen to the boy, and it's making me crazy."

"Where is Caleb, anyway, with your dad?'

"Yes, he's had him out with the sheep since early this morning. I packed them a big lunch, and they took a quart of orange juice, of all things. My father says the boy needs all the vitamins he can get. We need to get some meat on him, he says. I don't see how orange juice is going to do it." She smiled in spite of herself. "He has taken quite a shine to that boy. Says he's smart as a whip and is already a big help with the sheep. He says the dog hasn't bitten him a single time, either, though the boy roughhouses with him constantly. The dog likes him, too, I guess."

Sue chuckled. "Well, that's quite something. Those old-time Navajo dogs like yours are known to be biters. My dad says we used to have one, and it was constantly trying to bite me on the ass and herd me around."

Lucy took a long last drink of her coffee. "I don't know what to think really. I guess I was just wondering if you had heard anything from the boys or not."

"Not yet I haven't, but you know a lot of the places up there are hard to get out of, communications wise. I'm sure they'll get in touch when they can." Sue really wasn't sure how likely it would be for them to get in touch. Those two seemed to forget everything else when they were off together. It had been just the same in high school.

Lucy picked up her keys and stood to go. "Hey, I really appreciate you taking time out to talk. I expect we will get through this just fine."

Sue nodded and followed her out the door. "I'll let you know if I hear anything." She almost said "Keep an eye on that kid" but thought better of it. Outside, a little dirt storm was blowing up, and they each ran for their trucks with one hand on their hair.

~~~~~~~

Seventy-five-year-old Paul T'Sosi and six-year-old Caleb Begay sat under a shaggy barked cedar tree, overlooking the *hogan* and beyond—clear to the state highway. "Want some more orange juice?" the old man asked. "This stuff is good for you—it will make hair on your chest."

The boy looked at the old man. He had never seen an Indian with hair on his chest and was thinking Paul might be teasing him. "Have you got hair on your chest?" he wanted to know.

"Not yet, I haven't, but when we finish this orange juice, I might." He took a drink from the open jug and looked down at his shirtfront. "I can't wait to see if I've got any hair on my chest tomorrow"

The boy nodded, finally taking the juice jug. He took a long swallow for a little boy. "We'll see who's got the most hair on his chest tomorrow," he declared, wiping his mouth on his sleeve.

Paul smiled but was thoughtfully watching a dark-colored SUV stopped by the side of the distant highway. There was nothing out of the ordinary about the vehicle except this was the second time it had passed by, stopping each time directly across from the single track running up to the camp. No one got out or even rolled down a window.

5

The Revelation

Hiram Buck's meeting had not gone well, and for good reason: not only had he failed to silence Charlie Yazzie, but now another key witness, Sally Klee, thought to be in their pocket, had gone missing. Also half their insurance, in the form of Sally's son, was in other hands. The heavyset man in the black suburban nervously fingered his bolo tie, telling Hiram he did not see how things could possibly be worse. He went on to say Hiram had one week to somehow realign the stars in their favor. It seemed funny talk to Hiram, but he got his meaning and brusquely assured the man things would be different going forward. His visitor now thought it a huge mistake—trusting Hiram to carry out this critical part of the plan—and was not hesitant in saying so.

"I expected a lot better from someone who came so highly recommended." He sniffed. "You're making me look bad...and I don't like it." He did not get out of the Suburban to say this, however, as Hiram's reputation for volatility, ending in violence, was well known.

Hiram, not used to being talked to in this fashion, put his two big hands on the windowsill and leaned forward. "How would you like me to jerk you out of there and kick your ass, little man?"

This outburst did nothing to allay the man's fear. He had made a bad choice in Hiram Buck. There was nothing for it now, however. Hiram Buck knew too much, and changing horses midstream was not an option, at least not yet.

Hiram knew there would be no money until the upcoming trial was decided. The one exception being that should Charlie Yazzie be eliminated once and for all, that portion of the funds would be instantly forthcoming. They had told him so several times. The man in the bolo tie wanted Hiram to focus his attentions on Charlie Yazzie.

As the Suburban spun out of the yard in a cloud of red dust, Hiram fell into a truly murderous rage, mentally cursing his nephew George Jim for this horrible predicament. Nevertheless, he knew this same nephew was now his chief hope of eliminating the Navajo investigator.

Hiram hardly had time to settle his nerves before the state brand inspector's truck pulled up the lane. "This is all I need right now!" he said, bracing for his second confrontation of the morning.

Brand Inspector Dan Cleaver was well acquainted with Hiram Buck and his clan and learned to keep a sharp eye on any paperwork involving the family. The matter of the questionable heifer Hiram tried to run through the sale barn earlier had piqued his interest right from the start. The paperwork stated Hiram raised the animal, and she did carry a somewhat botched Buck brand. Mistakes occur during branding, and brands do get mangled from time to time, but there was something about this one that just didn't set right with the brand inspector. He had been a brand inspector for a long time and knew what he knew.

"Morning, Hiram! Didn't Aida Winters tell you I was looking for you about that heifer?"

Hiram stared at the brand inspector with a blank look on his face. "I haven't seen that woman in weeks. We're not exactly on the best of terms."

"Well anyway, I've got a heifer down at the sale barn that I've got a few questions on."

"Yeah, I saw she got a pass for brand inspection. What didn't you like about it." Hiram knew exactly what Dan did not like about it but played dumb, even knowing the inspector knew better.

Dan Cleaver looked him in the eye for a long moment and said nothing.

"Let me get my tally book," Hiram said at last. "I can show you exactly what mother cow it was out of and when she was dropped."

Dan was sure Hiram would have doctored his books by now

and sighed, waving him up to the house. While Hiram fetched the records, Dan looked the place over as carefully as he could without appearing too obvious. He had the right to search the entire corrals and outbuildings should he see fit, but he was not inclined to raise a fuss quite yet.

Hiram came out with the tattered record book, already opened to the page in question. He had filled in all the pertinent information any breeder might note in such a record, but it did seem to Dan the entry was a bit wedged in between two previous entries, all of which meant nothing. Hiram was free to keep his records in any fashion that struck his fancy. Dan knew the mother cow Hiram listed was probably long gone. The Bucks had shed all their cattle over the last six months. It was well known in those parts.

The inspector thought Hiram a little nervous, though the man was certainly no stranger to brand inquiries and was even accustomed to coming out on top in these encounters. None of his neighbors ever admitted to missing any stock. Wherever Hiram was coming up with these cows, it wasn't nearby.

Dan decided to change tack. "Well, I see Aida finally got that sorrel horse of yours," he said nonchalantly, pretending to study the tally book, but watching Hiram from under the brim of his hat.

Hiram was a little taken aback by this news of his horse and not just a little displeased. "You don't say?" He spit in the dirt of the yard. "I hope she likes him as well as I did,"

Dan Cleaver saw he struck a nerve and smiled to himself. "Oh, I don't expect she'll have a chance to find out if she likes him. She sold him right off the grounds for a nice profit to some Navajo law officer from Shiprock." He could see a twitch begin in Hiram's left eye, a trait several of the Buck family displayed when aggravated.

Pressing his advantage, the brand inspector became more direct. "I'm going to hold that heifer until I can look into this a little further." Then a parting shot. "Don't even think about picking her up until I contact you personally." With that, Dan handed Hiram back his tally book and turned to his truck.

"What was that Navajo law's name. Do you remember?"

"Yazzie," Dan threw back over his shoulder. "His name was Yazzie!"

~~~~~~~

George Jim, just at dawn, moved up the hillside toward the timbered ridge that lead, eventually, to Aida Winter's property. There was a spring high up on the ridge, and of late it had become the watering place for a very old mule deer buck. A buck he'd been keeping track of for some weeks now as it ranged back and forth over the two ranches. It was easy to spot with its off-side, drop-tine antler. It had only two tines on each side, showing the regression of age. After a time, a mule deer buck may not add points to its antlers. Worn teeth and poor nutrition can actually cause less growth each year. Although the spread may continue to widen and the bases thicken, the rack itself grows less impressive. It's extraordinarily difficult for a buck to reach this age at all. Some are surprised to find the venison from one of these old bucks more tender and flavorful than that of a younger more vigorous animal. Such old bucks keep mostly to themselves and no longer feel the need to pursue the does or run with the younger bucks. An old deer spends his time resting, conserving critical fat reserves, and avoiding confrontations.

George Jim kept a close eye on this particular deer for some time and thought now, in the flush of spring feed, a good time to take him. There was little feed on the overgrazed Buck property, but Aida's place was rife with fresh growth. As he eased across the hillside, he suddenly intersected tracks which led back down toward his own place—man tracks. Two men, it appeared, had gone down the draw, returning within hours.

Kit Carson once said a *Ute* Indian could track a piss-ant across a rockslide. The *Ute* steadfastly refused to trade their hunting skills for the plow. This fact had been pointed out to the government in 1879 by the massacre of Indian Agent Nathan Meeker and his staff at the White River Agency. Meeker thought to plow up the *Ute's* racetrack, which was their main source of entertainment. The ensuing rampage by the *Ute* not only meant the demise of the agency but the near total annihilation of a detachment of U.S. Cavalry sent to teach the *Ute* a lesson. There were yet those among the *Ute* who retained the instinct for such things. In the service, George Jim had been much in demand as a forward scout, as well as a sniper. The military generally thinks all Indians are natural born trackers and scouts. In the case of George Jim, they were proven right.

As George Jim studied the tracks, he became certain they did not belong to anyone he knew. Aida often came to check the small section of her fence on the ridge, making sure George or Hiram didn't let the fence down so their scraggly cows could get a free bellyful of grass. These were not Aida's tracks. Something about them told him it might not even be whites. To his way of thinking, these tracks stayed too much to the cover to be whites. The tracks were at least twenty-four hours old. The slight wind erosion on both sides of the prints made this clear. Afternoon winds sweeping up the ridge the afternoon before and then the downward flow of the night winds showed a near equal blurring of both edges of the track. Reading sign in this dry country was more challenging than most other environments. One almost had to grow up here to interpret the powdery soil. He followed the trail up the ridge to the fence line and then beyond. He could plainly see where someone had hidden two horses in the trees on Aida's land. Both horses wore shoes, but one was very freshly shod, within days he thought. It was this horse that showed a peculiar gait. It was vaguely familiar, yet he could not quite put his finger on it. He continued along the trail until he was certain. The riders had come from Aida Winters' home place.

As he turned to retrace his steps, the drop horned buck stood perfectly still and only a short distance away. The sun edged up over the ridge as George Jim raised his rifle to examine the buck through the scope and then centered the crosshairs. The safety was already off; solitary hunters, trained in the pursuit of other men, know the split-second warning in clicking it off could mean the difference between life and death.

George Jim was trained in making split-second decisions, decisions that might incur serious consequences. He lowered the bolt action .270 and cautiously began making his way off the ridge. The shot might have been heard from Aida's place. Ordinarily, he would not have cared. Aida didn't hear that well in any case. Now, however, she might have company who could hear. That threw a whole new slant on the matter. A person who makes a habit of hunting out of season has good reason to consider such things.

George Jim eased his way down through the final fringe of oak brush above his ramshackle trailer. That's when he saw Hiram's green pickup truck pulled right up to the built-on porch of the trailer. His uncle was sitting in the shade in the aluminum lawn chair that was missing one arm. Even from this distance George could tell by his body language that Hiram was in a temper. All his life he had been afraid of Hiram and, truth be told, still was. For the second time that day, he raised his rifle and studied a target through the scope. It would make his life so much easier. Yet, once again, he lowered the Winchester in deference to good judgment and common sense. He thought about just hiding there in the brush until Hiram went away, but he needed a drink of water, and Hiram showed no sign of leaving. George Jim swallowed hard and slipped on down to the edge of the clearing.

Hiram spotted him immediately and called loudly from the porch. "Get your ass down here, George!" He stood glowering at the younger man as he approached. "Where in hell have you been? I've been waiting since daylight!"

"I was up there trying to get a buck!" George yelled back, though he was nearly to the porch now and he thought to himself, "I could have got two bucks this morning, by God."

Hiram spit for the yard but hit the porch railing instead. Wiping his mouth on the back of his hand, he shook his head. "Well, forget about deer. We've got bigger fish to fry." He tried to keep his voice conciliatory. "I found out that law, Charlie Yazzie, is up in this country again...somewhere. All we have to do is find him." He looked George up and down, noting the camo paint on his face and hands. This boy was still out there, he thought. The crazy bastard.

George Jim set his rifle up against the porch railing and walked over to the water barrel by the door. He pulled out a cool dipperfull of water, hauled from Hiram's well. "You say he's up here again?"

"Yes." Hiram now carefully enunciated his words. "I said he's up here again." His nephew seemed closer to the edge every time he saw him. "The brand inspector dropped by yesterday morning about that heifer we rebranded. Said Yazzie bought my horse from Aida on Sunday."

George Jim let the cool water trickle slowly down his throat and placed the dipper back in the barrel. The barrel was wrapped in wet burlap bags that felt almost cold to the touch. He wiped his hands on the wet sacking and held them to his face before turning back to Hiram. "You say…he bought your horse from Aida?"

Hiram's eyes went flat, and he was about to scream. "Yes, you dumb sonofabitch. He bought my horse!" But something about the expression on George Jim's face made the words catch in his throat. What he saw was an excruciating sense of enlightenment. The young ex-soldier sat himself down on the porch steps like a sack of potatoes. Hiram watched closely, fearing he had pushed him too far. He was clearly on the edge.

After a long moment staring across the barren yard, a thin smile crossed George Jim's wide features. He knew now what had seemed familiar about that horse's tracks: it had been favoring it's off hind foot. "Uncle," he murmured softly, "I believe I know where to find that Navajo."

~~~~~~~

Caleb Begay, though only six years old, had seen more than most his age. He had endured more trouble and neglect for one thing. He faulted no one in this regard, having no yardstick with which to measure any sort of life other than his own. He had no reason to believe there was anything better. He and his sister Ida were, of necessity, self-reliant and could fend for themselves should need be. When he was very small, he vaguely recalled Thomas Begay being around a good deal, and things seemed better then, at least for him and Ida. Thomas liked children and Caleb and his sister in particular for some reason. He wished Ida were here at this place with him. He missed his sister. They had been together ever since he could remember, and though she was only a year older, she had always taken care of him to the extent of her young ability. He wondered where she could be and when she would be coming back. She would like it here at Thomas and Lucy's, he thought. She would like the old man, too. Paul T'Sosi could relate to children in a way other grownups seldom did.

This morning Caleb rose extra early and went to sing his blessing song to the sunrise before making his morning run. This was a very old ritual. Traditional *Dinè* boys and girls learned it from an early age. He slipped off into the sand wash and ran toward the sun until his lungs burned and his legs were shaky and weak. As he sank to his knees in the sand, he noticed the dog loping along his back trail. The dog didn't rush to jump on him, wagging and licking, as some dogs might do. This dog stopped a few feet away, crouching, tail slowly waving back and forth, watching this boy who had become a new part of their lives. The boy stared hard at the dog, causing him to lower his head and crawl forward to Caleb's outstretched hand.

The morning was cool, but the run had brought a fine bead of perspiration to the boy's upper lip. He stood and the dog stood with him, both savoring the morning breeze, fresh with the smell of the desert.

The dog raised his head and lifted his nose to the air currents, reading the stories they brought. He stiffened slightly when he smelled the rabbit. The boy saw him hesitate only an instant before leaping ahead and around the corner of the wash. By the time Caleb reached him, the dog had already caught the rabbit and was giving it a final shake. Navajo dogs, like Navajo boys, are a self-reliant breed used to rustling for themselves. In bygone days, when times were hard, these dogs had been instrumental in the very survival of the *Dinè*. Caleb advanced on the dog, though it growled deep in its throat and gripped the rabbit tighter. Ordinarily, the dog would not willingly part with the rabbit to anyone but the old man or possibly Lucy should he be in a generous mood. He would not have given the rabbit to Thomas under any circumstances. This boy, however, had worked his magic on the dog as he had on the people. Finally, the dog dropped the rabbit on the ground, allowing the boy to pick it up. Caleb told the dog in Navajo he had done well, and this rabbit would be good for their breakfast. He thought Lucy might be persuaded to help them cook it. The old man told him that one day he would teach him to start a fire and fix a rabbit himself, but so far a rabbit had not presented itself. Now he would see.

As the dog and then the boy, dragging the rabbit, climbed up out of the sand wash, they saw they had come nearly to the highway. They looked around somewhat surprised at how far from the *hogan* they now were. They immediately noticed a black vehicle parked along the edge of the road leading to their camp. The door opened and someone appeared to be getting out when a cloud of dust came boiling down the lane from the *Hogan*—it was Lucy Tallwoman in the blue diesel truck.

The figure in the car quickly closed the door and spun the tires getting back up on the highway. Lucy pulled up beside Caleb and, without taking her eyes off the retreating Suburban, said calmly, "Get in the back; I don't want any fleas in this new truck." This made sense to the boy as he knew rabbits often had fleas. At least he thought she was referring to the rabbit, but looked suspiciously at the dog as well. There was no tailgate on the truck, and the dog jumped up in the bed, followed by the boy, who first threw in the rabbit and then pulled himself up into the bed, using the hitch as a step.

Lucy had arisen to find the boy's cot empty, and while both she and her father approved of his running to meet the dawn, she felt uneasy awakening to find him already gone. Always before, she was first up and able to watch the boy run. This morning he chose the wash, and that prevented her seeing him.

When they arrived back at the *hogan*, the dog jumped out first then the boy dragging the rabbit with him. Lucy looked at the rabbit approvingly. "That is a nice young cottontail. Do you want him for your breakfast?"

The old man came around the sheep corrals and saw the rabbit. "Whoa! It looks like we are having 'gah' for breakfast!" using the Navajo word for rabbit. He took the rabbit from the boy then noticed his daughter looking off down the road, shading her eyes with one hand. "What?" he asked.

"Someone was getting out of a car down there at the highway when I picked these two up," she said with a push of her lips toward the boy and dog.

"Black Suburban?"

"Yes. I'm thinking we should not let this boy out of our sight for a while."

Paul T'Sosi nodded his head, motioning for the boy to come along with him to the edge of the compound. The boy and dog followed closely, not wanting to miss a single step in fixing this rabbit. The dog, knowing what was coming, kept his eyes on Caleb. This boy seemed to be of some value to these people and, like the sheep, would require watching.

The old man first stepped on the rabbits head with one foot. Holding the hind feet, he gave a quick jerk, leaving the head on the ground. He then pulled out his pocketknife and, opening the small blade, made an incision across the skin of the rabbits back. Inserting his two index fingers in the cut, he slowly pulled the skin off in both directions. The boy's eyes grew large, but the dog was unimpressed, having seen Paul pull a rabbit's pants off many times. Paul inserted just the tip of the blade and ran it the length of the paunch, taking care not to nick the intestines. Holding the rabbit by the hind feet, he gave a quick sling of the carcass, flinging the entrails over the edge of the wash. The entire process had taken less than two minutes, and the rabbit was totally clean. He need only cut the feet off to make it ready for the pot.

In olden days his people had roasted rabbits on a green stick over the embers of a fire or added them to a pot for stew—those lucky enough to have a pot. Paul now liked his rabbits cut up like a chicken and rolled in flour to fry. If Lucy had a little canned milk, she might make some cream gravy as well. He doubted his people could have made it in those long-ago times without rabbits for food, blankets, and clothing.

Paul let Caleb carry the rabbit back to Lucy to cook, to show he had been the provider. Paul acknowledged the dog's part in the thing with a pat on the head. The dog would have to be satisfied with the leftovers when they were finished, provided there were any leftovers. If not, he would have to go catch himself another rabbit. There seemed to be plenty of rabbits this year. It was a tradeoff dogs had come to terms with thousands of years ago. Should the people kill something big (a deer or later a sheep or goat or even a beef) the dog would receive his share. It had worked this way for a very long time, and both parties found it equitable or at least preferable to going it alone. Navajo dogs were free to go whenever they felt the inclination. It was an option few chose.

That night, when the boy was asleep, Lucy whispered to her father, "I don't think this boy is safe here anymore." She looked over at the sleeping child. "I'm thinking maybe we should take him away from here. Maybe take him up north to Thomas's Uncle Johnny at Navajo Mountain."

Paul T'Sosi considered this. "Well, John Nez is the boy's blood relative, and I am sure he would be willing to take him in. Still, I would hate to take him so far away without Thomas knowing about it."

It was unlike the old man to be so solicitous of Thomas's feelings. Lucy felt he had grown so fond of the boy he hated to see him go. She knew her father thought he could keep Caleb from harm, but this morning's episode made it clear another plan was called for. She thought maybe she should talk to Sue Hanagarni about it. Possibly she could get word to Charlie and Thomas and see what they thought. Thomas would soon have to take an active part in the raising of this boy, and the sooner he began expressing an opinion, the better.

~~~~~~~~

Lucy Tallwoman left a message for Thomas's uncle, John Nez, at the chapter house at Navajo Mountain. She only said he was needed immediately.

She knew she could not leave her father there alone in order to deliver the boy to Navajo Mountain herself, especially so soon after Paul's recent illness. Then, of course, there were the sheep. Always there were the sheep.

Early the following morning John Nez and his white friend, anthropologist Marissa Key, pulled up in front of Lucy's *hogan*. John had driven all night to get there despite Marissa saying they could wait till the next morning. She had hardly had time to get any clothes together for the two of them, she said.

Lucy was a little nervous when she saw Marissa had come along. She didn't know what an educated white woman would think of their more humble way of living out there on Tortilla Flats, as her father liked to refer to it. Then she thought of the new generator Thomas bought when he went back to work and felt better. The generator was exactly like the one Marissa had at John Nez's place up at Navajo Mountain. Lucy didn't have a propane kitchen range like Marissa, but they were working on that. Thomas said they needed to step into the twenty-first century at some point, and this was as good a time as any.

He had said, "When those people up at Navajo Mountain start getting more modern stuff than we have down here, it is a wakeup call!"

Lucy reminded him that Marissa was the only one up there who had much in the way of modern conveniences, and she had bought them all herself.

"Well then," Thomas had stated, "it is a wakeup call for all those other people up at Navajo Mountain, too."

John Nez and Marissa settled their belongings in the "summer *hogan*"—just a brush arbor really, often the focal point of family life in the warmer summer months. Lucy usually set up her loom there in the dog days of summer. The brush shelter made for handy guest accommodations too, given good weather.

"This is sort of like camping out, isn't it," Marissa whispered, looking doubtfully at the army cots along the sparse, brushy walls.

John just looked at her. "You will be surprised how nice it is sleeping out here." He hoped she would not insist on going to town for accommodations—that would be an embarrassment. "You can see the stars right through the roof," he offered. He often thought white women made for troublesome companions. He sometimes wondered if the wear and tear on his head was worth it.

They all gathered there in the shade and sipped the sodas John Nez brought in his cooler. The boy was called from his work of teaching the dog to retrieve a stick. Secretly, the dog thought he was teaching the boy to throw it. They both came to the call rather reluctantly as each felt himself just on the verge of success.

John Nez watched the boy approach and nodded approvingly. "That's Thomas's boy alright; Thomas looked just like that when he was little."

This was not particularly good news for some who knew Thomas best. Old Paul T'Sosi, for one, hoped the boy would not follow too closely in his father's footsteps and vowed privately to set a stronger example himself.

After the boy had been introduced to his new relative and to Marissa, he was allowed to return to his schooling of the dog. He had not spoken a word during the introductions, but John Nez thought this was all right. A boy should come along at his own pace, he said.

After the boy had gone outside, John Nez started off the conversation regarding Caleb's safety with the thought they should not be too hasty. Whisking the boy away to another strange place and people he hardly knew might not be the best thing. He thought the boy had already had enough of that.

Lucy wondered if this was John Nez talking, or could it be Marissa. She had noticed in the past that Marissa was quite happy with her life up at Navajo Mountain just the way it was.

Paul T'Sosi, however, was pleased at this turn in the conversation, preferring to keep the boy right here in camp. He felt he was already making progress educating Caleb in old traditions and certain other things he might well need to know someday.

"I have said all along the boy would be best off here with us," the old man said, leaning forward in his chair. "I know we are not his blood, but his father will no doubt be back soon. The boy belongs with his father since his mother and sister are nowhere to be found."

Lucy recounted for them the series of incidents that caused her initial concern, ending with the day before when the black car parked at the end of the road. "I think whoever was in that car meant to take Caleb!" she said firmly, crossing her arms over her chest. Lucy's body language told Marissa she was no longer open to discussion.

John Nez looked thoughtful for a moment. "What about this: how about me and Marissa hang around for a few days to give the boy some added protection, just until Thomas gets back. It will show anyone watching the family is on guard. This thing might, pretty quick, sort itself out."

Marissa spoke for the first time. "I have been dying to see Lucy's work on the loom and get her ideas for the chapter I'm writing about Navajo weaving."

John nodded, adding, "We have been wanting to come down for a visit anyway. It will give us all a chance to get to know one another better and maybe figure something out about the boy." He paused, looking from one to the other. "Hopefully, Thomas will be heard from soon. Rightfully, as has been said, he is the one to make this decision."

Everyone had now been offered a chance to speak their mind on the matter, and to their way of thinking, this constituted an in-depth discussion, which in time should lead to some sort of solution. Navajos are not ones to talk a thing to death.

~~~~~~~

Sue Hanagarni sat at her desk in somewhat of a quandary. She'd been keeping a close eye on Pete Fish after what he had said.

He had asked her out for the third time that week and she, as usual, politely refused, hoping each time would be the last.

Pete Fish, however, was not to be denied. She finally told him she didn't think Charlie would like it if they went out.

Pete Fish dropped his head and started away from her desk but suddenly turned and hissed under his breath, "Charlie Yazzie may not always be around, you know! You might do well to reconsider your options." With that he stormed out of the office, leaving several of the older women exchanging looks and casting sideways glances at Sue.

The last time she and Charlie talked, he asked her who had ordered him to go to Blanding for the deposition. It seemed like a petty thing at the time, but it played on her mind over the last few days, and more and more she wondered if Pete Fish had just been trying to clear the playing field, or was there more to it than that. She couldn't help wonder if Charlie told her everything about his trip and finding the boy.

Pete Fish's comment about considering her options struck a nerve. Apparently, even he thought the chances of her and Charlie being a sure thing was not a sure thing. Sue was not one to shilly-shally. She liked to know exactly where she stood and resolved to find out when Charlie returned.

She was aware that her aging parents were a further issue. The question must have crossed his mind of how she would manage to continue caring for them should she and Charlie find their own place in the country. She was almost certain they could not afford a large enough place for her parents to live with them, assuming Charlie would agree to it at all. Her parents were quite old, having had Sue late in life when little hope remained of having a child at all.

Maybe Charlie thought he could wait them out. They had been sick a very long time and certainly would not last forever. Sue's mind hit overdrive now, and no possibility seemed too bizarre to consider. Sue knew the old people worried about her and hoped she would find a husband while they were still alive to see it. They thought the world of Charlie and felt he would be a perfect match for their often headstrong daughter.

Just the previous morning, she found an automated message on her line when she opened the switchboard. She had to run the volume up considerably to make out the words.

"Hi, Sue. I'm calling from Monticello. It's the only place high enough to get out to the radio towers and…." The message faded and static crackled. "…northern Utah. Should be back in a …" Again his voice was gone, and though the message ran for another full minute, she couldn't decipher any more of it.

"…should be back in a…?" What? In an hour? A day? A week? She wasn't at all sure she was ready for a life with so adventurous a man. Charlie was up there on his own, taking vacation time to help Thomas find his daughter. She admired him for helping their old friend, but Thomas had already nearly gotten Charlie killed. Being a lawyer was supposed to be a safe, prosperous occupation. So far this was not the case.

Later, as Sue walked past the water cooler, she heard one of the women ask another, "Did you see that new car Pete Fish bought?"

The other woman nodded. "Pretty fancy if you ask me. I didn't know he made that kind of money."

"Too bad some people around here can't see an opportunity when it comes knocking." The older woman said this loud enough for Sue to hear. Sue could feel the heat rise to her face, but she knew what was right for her and didn't care what anyone else might think. These old women did not know everything.

6

The Ute

When the White River Ute band wore out their welcome with the massacre of Nathan Meeker and his minions (after wiping out Major Thornburg's cavalry unit, sent to prevent it) the United States Government was provided just the excuse needed to remove them from that country entirely. They were taken from their more desirable Colorado lands and relocated to the barren and desolate reaches of Utah's Uinta and Ouray Reserve. Many thought it poetic justice that the Mormons would now have to deal with this polygamous and irascible band of Indians.

Charlie and Thomas were several hours into their long drive up to the Ute Reservation in northeastern Utah when they found it necessary to stop in Monticello for fuel. Waiting for the tank to fill, Thomas wondered out loud, "Are you allowed to take this truck out of state?"

"As long as it's one of the Four Corners states or anywhere there's a piece of Navajo reservation."

"This will be about the farthest I've ever been out of New Mexico." Thomas scratched his head. "I'm pretty sure it is."

"Well, I doubt you will see anything new where we're going. I haven't been there myself, but I've heard the stories." The pump shut off and Charlie frowned at the price. "But then we're not up here on vacation, you know." He opened the truck door before adding, "If Hiram's relations up there have Ida, we'll have our work cut out for us getting her back."

Thomas followed along into the convenience store, and as Charlie paid for the gas, Thomas picked up a dozen chocolate donuts. They were his favorites, and while nearly every store carried them, he always felt lucky when he found them. "A lot of times they are sold out," he assured his friend.

Charlie's thoughts drifted back to Aida talking about the paperwork Hiram delivered on cows he sometimes brought down from his relatives up on the Uinta. It hadn't taken Charlie long to decide a talk with the brand inspector might be in order.

Brand inspectors mostly work out of their trucks. They keep no regular office other than sale barn restaurants. When Thomas and Charlie stopped by his house the day before, Brand Inspector Dan Cleaver was fairly accommodating for a man in the middle of his breakfast. He pulled out several fat record books and made quite a fuss thumbing through the entries. His search turned up several names on the transfer papers from Hiram's relatives. Hiram brought down several batches of stock that year. "He picks up some pretty scrappy stuff up there, then brings them down here to feed out and run through the sale. He starts 'em out on government grass—a BLM lease his bunch has up by Bluff." He smiled. "Then tries to finish them out down here on his own place." He shook his head. "The feed on his place has been so poor of late he can't be making much on them now." He looked thoughtful for a moment. "Unless, of course, someone's running a long iron up there." A grim smile crossed his face. "I've been trying to figure it out for a while now. Even talked to the Utah brand inspector a couple of times. He covers a lot of ground—big as some states, he claims. He doesn't really have time to track anything down for me."

Charlie copied down the information Dan had on record and took the name of the Utah brand inspector as well.

In parting, Dan pulled no punches. "That's a pretty rough crowd up there, Yazzie; smart too. I doubt they'll be impressed with a Navajo Nation badge." He coughed discreetly. "I'd step lightly if you know what I mean."

Charlie, with a serious nod, thanked him for the information. He told the brand inspector they would let him know if they turned up anything that might interest him.

Back in the truck Thomas went a little shifty eyed. "Is the revolver still in the glove box?" He opened the little drop down door and was relieved to see not only the .38 but a brand new box of cartridges as well.

Charlie grimaced and rolled his eyes when he saw the look on Thomas's face.

It was nearly dark when they pulled into Roosevelt, Utah, and divvied up for a cheap motel room.

The next morning they looked up the Utah State Brand Inspector, a no-nonsense sort who Charlie figured for a Mormon. He knew most of the good state jobs, in these isolated areas of Utah were generally held by Mormons. The man was not used to seeing Navajos so far north but took it in stride as they laid out their reason for being there. They told him the Colorado Brand Inspector in Cortez mentioned he might be able to help them. Their main objective was to locate Hiram Buck's relatives who had been supplying him stock. The brand inspector, a big man, who looked remarkably like John Wayne, but whose name was Tim Nordstrom, went through his records and came up with a few names and addresses. Charlie noticed he already had notes stuck on those pages.

"These ought to help," he said handing them the notes. "These people up here don't talk to strangers a whole hell of a lot, especially ones carrying a badge." He looked at the two men with a quizzical expression. "What do you want with these people, if you don't mind me asking? The brand inspector down at Cortez asked me to keep an eye on Buck's people…but I'm only one man." He added, "These particular folks are not easy to keep track of. They move around a lot and there's a lot of 'under the table' deals, if you get my drift."

Thomas thought he sounded exactly like John Wayne when he said this last and had to look twice to make sure he was serious. Thomas had always thought well of John Wayne regardless of the number of Indians he killed in his movies. Thomas had known many Navajos who had dressed up as other tribes and appeared in Wayne movies filmed on the reservation and thereabouts. They all liked him immensely, and many had their pictures taken with him. Those pictures made interesting conversation pieces at the local bars and were sometimes good for a free drink.

As they took their leave, Tim Nordstrom had an afterthought.

"There is one other place you might want to check: Tom's Market just west of town. You passed it coming in. Tom Brawly has run that store twenty years; grew up here; caters mostly to Indians. He claims not to care for them…and they don't trust him, but they damn sure do a lot of business together. No one knows more about the locals than him." He paused, looking directly at Charlie. "These *Ute* up here are mostly good folks…just trying to get along like the rest of us. But there's always a few," he indicated the notes Charlie held in his hand, "who make all the rest look bad."

Charlie thought Tom Brawly's store would be a good place to start. As they pulled up in front of the building, he took note of several older Indian men sitting on a bench beside the door. He remembered back to his childhood and the trading post near his grandmother's place. Oftentimes, men would be found sitting on a bench outside due to being barred from the store for drunkenness or some other breach of decorum. Their wives would still be allowed in to shop, but the men would remain outside talking. Sometimes after a long while, a year maybe, a man might be allowed back in the store…but not always.

The *Utes* outside the store saw the Navajo tribal emblem on the truck and, looking away, nudged one another. Thomas, who was munching a chocolate donut, looked down at the box and counted those that were left. There were five. He had eaten seven donuts since he'd bought them the previous day. He was pacing himself in case the stores up here didn't carry this brand—the one with the little redheaded girl in pigtails on the box. Charlie wouldn't eat them after Marissa told them these donuts had wax added to the chocolate coating to prevent melting in warm weather. Now, when Thomas took time to really savor these donuts, he thought he could detect that wax on the back of his tongue. He wished Marissa hadn't mentioned the wax. Not that it really mattered; these were still his favorites.

When Charlie and Thomas entered the store, they could see what attracted the local *Ute*. You could not have assembled a better range of stock for Indians, to their way of thinking. There were groceries of all kinds, including a large variety of snacks, canned goods, and dry foods that would last a long time without refrigeration. Piles of Levi's and jackets were on a long table against the back wall. There was the hardware and ammunition section and another for saddles and tack, including a good selection of used saddles and even a few horse-related health products. Thomas naturally gravitated to that area of the store.

Charlie made his way back to the meat counter where a small rotund man in a white apron was cutting up what appeared to be a mutton quarter. Since this was the only store person in evidence, other than the old woman at the checkout, he assumed this was Tom Brawly. Charlie could see he was quite familiar with the mechanics of his work and didn't quit cutting as he looked up when Charlie approached the counter.

"What can I do for you?" the man asked in a not unfriendly way. He gave Charlie a quick second look and knew immediately he was not from around there. He laid the knife down and, wiping his hands on his fresh apron, came around the cutting block to the counter.

Charlie flashed his badge too quickly for the man to read and did not identify himself further. "Do you know any of these people," he asked, passing the man the notepaper containing the names and addresses the brand inspector had given him.

The store man gave the names a brief look. "Maybe," he said. "What did they do now?"

Obviously, their reputation preceded them. "I don't know that they have done anything as yet," Charlie answered. "I'm just running down some information we need to clear up an unrelated matter." This was as ambiguous an answer as he could come up with on the spur of the moment.

"Anything specific?"

The man behind the counter grew cautious now but was obviously curious and inclined to help, if Charlie was any judge, though Charlie had proven on several occasions he was not.

Thomas watched from across the room as he felt the fender leather on a beautifully kept antique Heiser saddle. The old woman at the checkout counter kept a close eye on him as he moved from saddle to saddle, though he seriously doubted he could smuggle one of these saddles out under his shirt. He could see Charlie and the meat man were having quite a conversation. Finally, he observed Charlie taking back his address notes and raising a hand to the man in farewell.

Thomas met him halfway to the front of the store.

"Could you help me steal one of those saddles over there?" he grinned. "That old woman at the register is sure I can do it, and I would just like to see if she's right."

Charlie smiled and shook his head, and they made for the door just as a group of younger men in baseball caps turned backwards jostled through the opening. They silently looked Thomas and Charlie over. They knew from the pickup outside they were Navajos.

The tallest of them came forward and pushed his face close to Thomas. "You boys are a little out of your hood, aren't you?"

Thomas grinned. "What makes you think so?"

Charlie smiled as well. Thomas might not look it, but he could fight. He avoided it whenever he could talk his way out, and he usually could, but when he saw he couldn't, he didn't hesitate to engage. When he did engage, it was with a fury. Charlie saw him fight several times in high school and was impressed. He knew Thomas had later learned a great deal more about fighting in the back alley bars of Farmington and Gallup. He had made somewhat of a reputation for himself among the town Indians. He might be afraid of *Yeenaaldiooshii* but he wasn't afraid of this kind of trash. Charlie could tell Thomas was gearing up, and it wouldn't take much to set him off. That would not be a good thing.

Charlie stepped toward the boys and flashed the magic badge. The leader barely glanced at it before stepping back and making way for them. Thomas smiled at the young tough as he passed but said nothing.

Back in the truck Charlie laughed. "You were ready to rock, huh, *hastiin*?"

Thomas grinned, rubbing his knuckles. "They were just punks. Out of the four of them, only one had any fight, and it wasn't the one doing the talking either. It never is."

Charlie laughed again. He could see the four *Utes* watching them from the window. Those boys just narrowly missed getting tutored.

The first name on Hiram Buck's short list of relatives proved to be an old woman living by herself, it seemed. Charlie doubted, however, the cinder block, government-housing unit would have been given out to a single old woman.

When she answered the door, she immediately pulled back and looked at them as though they might be from another planet. "Who are you?" she asked, noting the tribal pickup behind them.

Charlie didn't bother with the badge as he thought her already intimidated by the truck.

"We're looking for a young girl who disappeared down south of here." He could see her hesitate.

"I don't know nothing about no girl," she offered in a low, raspy voice.

"Thomas stepped forward. "She's my daughter we're looking for. Her name is Ida. She is related to Hiram Buck from down by Cortez. She's only seven years old. We have good reason to believe she's up here on the Uinta."

Charlie noticed a glimmer of something cross the woman's face at the mention of Hiram Buck, and he quickly pressed the point.

"Someone is going to be in a lot of trouble if we don't find that girl!" And then he said, "Federal kidnapping charges may be filed if we don't find her first." And finally in a more friendly tone, "You don't want the FBI up here poking around, do you?"

The old woman was clearly alarmed at the mention of kidnapping charges. "Well, my boys didn't have nothing to do with it!" She looked fearfully from one to the other. "My boys wouldn't have nothing to do with anything like that."

"Who are your boys?"

The woman tried to shut the door, but Thomas was too quick for her and stuck his foot in the opening.

"We just need to ask them a few questions is all," Charlie insisted. "We have a list here of Hiram Buck's relatives. One of them is going to talk to us, and the one that does might get off lightly in case of charges!"

"My boys didn't do nothing. They're not that kind of boys." The old woman was clearly worried now. "My Billy and Jim don't live here right now. They are at cow camp up on Sarvis Creek. My boys have chil'ren of their own, They wouldn't take no little girl. They already got plenty girls."

In the end, the old woman had given them some rather vague directions to the cow camp, and after hearing how isolated it was, Charlie thought they might be on to something. The old woman stood at the crack in the door, watching the two Navajos drive back out to the highway. "Those two better hope they don't find my boys out there on the mountain," she said to herself with a grim smile of satisfaction.

Thomas was getting excited now too, and as they headed back into the high country, he watched the side roads for the National Forest sign the old woman mentioned.

"I wish we had brought those horses; they might come in real handy up in this country."

"Well, I doubt they'd stay in the back of this truck without a stock-rack or a trailer to put them in."

"Aida has an old oak stock rack in the back of her barn," Thomas remembered.

"I saw that. I figured on asking if it were for sale before we left. I hate to have to rent a trailer to take those ponies home. Surely, we know someone with a trailer. I could check one out from one of the tribal agencies, but I hate to do that without a pretty good explanation." Charlie had clearly given this a lot of thought.

It hadn't even crossed Thomas's mind how they would get their new horses home. That was the difference between him and Charlie, he guessed—Charlie was a thinker, and he was a doer.

A Forest Service truck was parked at the turnoff to the creek. When they found it, a middle-aged man in a green shirt sat in the cab eating his lunch. He rolled down the window as they pulled alongside and said, "Howdy! You boys doing all right today?" He glanced at the logo on the truck and grinned. "You lost?"

Charlie smiled back. "Probably! We got some directions, but we're not sure how accurate they might be." He pointed up the road beside the creek. "Is there a cow camp up at the head of this creek?"

"Yes, yes there is. It's a good bit up the mountain, though, and gets pretty rough too. Are you sure you want to beat up that new Chevy?"

"We're looking for the Klee brothers. Is that their camp back in there?"

"It is for a fact," the man affirmed, "but unless you know 'em pretty well, they can be a bit ouchy. I wouldn't recommend just busting in on 'em, if you know what I mean."

"That's what we hear." Charlie agreed, grinning.

"I don't get back in there much anymore myself. Got tired of fighting with them," the worker admitted. "There's lots of people interested in 'em of late, but not many have the *cojones* to deal with 'em direct. Nearly the whole clan lives back up there for the summer—just like the old days." He thought for a bit. "I doubt they'd even come out in winter if the game didn't come down and leave 'em to starve." He chuckled. "I guess just about everybody wants a piece of those boys: brand inspector, game warden, and now you. I don't have any put-in with what goes on up there...and don't want any. As long as they get their cows off Forest Service lands in the fall when they're supposed to, I have no quarrel with them." He started to roll up his window but said in parting, "There's a fire trail up the other side of the creek about a quarter-mile that veers off to the left. If a person wanted to look the situation over, before jumping in, he could follow that track on around the top of a little knob across from their camp. Sorta' get the lay of the land, should he be of a mind."

Charlie thanked him for the information and on past the creek eased the truck up the steep and rocky service road, trying to avoid the worst of the chokecherry bushes reaching out to snag the paint.

Thomas frowned. "Maybe we should have checked out a couple of the other people on the list first."

Charlie reminded Thomas that there were only two other people on the list with the Klee name, and that was Billy and Jim Klee, and they all shared the old woman's address. *The butcher back in Roosevelt who looked at their list mentioned the Klee boys as likely candidates for chancy livestock dealings.* "Those two work off a tribal grazing permit from the Forest Service in the summer and have been selling butchered beef for years." It was hurting his trade, he confided. Not to mention their fellow tribesmen who were short cattle at the end of every season. It was about time something was done about it.

A number of *Ute* who ran cows up there knew about the Klee's but figured it was just the cost of doing business. They knew those people could and would cost them much more, should they make trouble for them.

Utes do not have an elaborate system of clans and ceremonies. In bygone days, *Hozo* did not enter into their more visceral culture. The *Ute* had their Bear Dance. It was their major ceremony. The grizzly bear was signal to that culture and was much venerated by all the bands of the tribe. The grizzly was gone now from those mountains but still lived on in the minds of the *Ute*.

As the truck began its torturous climb up the backside of the knob, Charlie glanced over at Thomas and ventured, "You don't look too happy, *hastiin*. Something on your mind?"

Thomas squinted one eye, looked off into the distance, then brushing his hair from his eyes, said softly, "Kinda odd that forest guy, sitting right there where we needed to turn off...and being so helpful and all. Probably nothing, I know, but still..."

Charlie let the pickup gear itself to a stop in the middle of the brushy track. He was learning to listen a little more closely now to his old friend. He sat there a moment drumming his fingers on the steering wheel. He himself was used to dealing with white people. The class of whites he had contact with were generally trustworthy. Thomas's street-smart life had left him with a somewhat more jaundiced view of the white world. For him, it had been a world that didn't include helpful officials.

Charlie frowned. "As long as we're being paranoid, I suppose Tom Brawly might well have tipped them off. He could have sent one of those young toughs from the store to warn them or maybe just made a phone call." He rubbed his forehead with the back of his hand and stared hard at Thomas. "Or maybe the brand inspector is in on it and is setting us up!"

Thomas was grinning now. "Okay, so I was thinking a little crazy. I'll try to concentrate on the facts. Now, what were those facts again?"

Charlie grinned back. "What we need to concentrate on is Hiram Buck and whoever he's working for." He nodded to himself thoughtfully. "The three major prosecution witnesses in the upcoming Greyhorse trial are you, me, and Sally. I believe they tried for me first, hoping to later buy you and Sally off through intimidation and money."

"Uh...what made them think they could buy me off...in your

professional opinion, of course?" Thomas had straightened up in his seat and was clearly incensed at the implication. He looked sideways out the window. "How much money do you think we're talking anyway?"

Charlie almost smiled. "Well, no offense my man, but there is your track record to consider. There are rich and powerful people behind this. Their lives are at stake here, and they are desperate. The Patsy Greyhorse murders proved they will stop at nothing!" He paused with a contemplative glance at Thomas. "They will do things the easy way if they can, but if not, they will do whatever they have to do." He went on, "They have only one major witness accounted for if they still have Sally Klee, though I'm beginning to wonder if that's the case."

Thomas shrugged. "Sally will run if she gets a chance. No doubt in my mind about that. But she does care for those kids, and she is smart in her own way. If I know her, she's doing some hard thinking right now."

Charlie looked up the rutted track before them and chewed his lip for a moment.

"Let's ease on up there and scope the place out." He pointed to the binoculars in the rack over the dash and went on, "I doubt we can sneak up on that camp in daylight. They know every rock and bush up here."

Thomas doubted they could sneak up on those people in the dark either but held his tongue.

Charlie knew his history when it came to the *Ute*: Since their beginning, the *Ute* survived by their wiles and ability to endure in this country before they had the horse. Afterward, they became the capable guardians of these vast mountain strongholds. Early trappers thought only fools would approach the *Ute* in these mountains with war on their mind. Only the Blackfoot and Crow, far to the north, were more feared by the early mountain men.

The *Ute*, when they came down to the plains to hunt buffalo, were called "black people." Their dark skin was possibly the result of high-altitude sun exposure, and the ten-thousand-year process of natural selection to protect against it.

~~~~~~~

The two Navajos lay perfectly still behind a light screen of scrub oak. It was a narrow ledge just off the top of the knob but afforded a good view of the Klee cow camp. The two passed the field glasses back and forth as they tried to commit every detail of the place to memory. The building was a low, ramshackle log structure from the early part of the century. Repairs over the decades had been minimal at best, yet the Klee's obviously still considered it a viable shelter.

A large iron caldron sat on a smoldering fire in the front yard, and two older women stood talking while they tended what was inside. Take away the modern clothes and the stock truck at the edge of the clearing and it could have been a scene from a hundred fifty years ago.

There was a holding pen connected to the side of the cabin and a larger corral encompassing a few scraggly Aspen trees. No horses or other stock could be seen and, strangely, no dogs either.

Several children played about the far edge of the compound with an older girl apparently in charge. There was no sign of men or even older boys.

"The men must be out on a war party," Thomas whispered, only half joking. He anxiously scanned the children and at first did not recognize his seven-year-old daughter who was dressed as a boy, her hair cropped short. Ida looked healthy and not at all worried. She probably thought she was just on a little vacation with her cousins.

Charlie felt Thomas tense up and for an instant thought he might break and run down there. He put a hand on Thomas's shoulder and held up a cautioning finger.

"Easy now, big guy," he said softly. "We need to think about this for a minute."

Thomas could barely contain himself at the sight of the girl. "There are no horses down there...or dogs. The men are out working stock, I think. It won't get any better than this. If we wait till dark, the men will be back, and it's going to mean a fight. We're only one gun."

"Well, ya know, we could just sneak back down the mountain and call in some real law."

"They've got a boy down that road watching. You can count on it." Thomas was adamant. "The law wouldn't get within a mile of this place without they whisk Ida back into the mountains. We'd play hell getting her back then."

Charlie hesitated, mulling over the many possibilities, ones he knew Thomas had not even considered. In the end, however, he concluded his friend was right. Now or never!

They moved back from the edge. "Work your way down into that little grove of evergreens by the creek," he told Thomas. "She knows you and won't put up much of a fuss when you grab her and make a run for it."

Charlie emphasized his next words. "Do Not Stop For Anything! Don't try to hide! These people know every inch up here. Head downstream the other side of the creek for about a quarter mile. I'll be waiting with the truck at that first big switchback! If I'm not there, head straight down the track. I'll pick you up one way or another." He paused to catch his breath. "Just give me a five-minute head start." He looked Thomas square in the eye. "Uh…if there is a boy watching down the road, he's likely to have a gun to signal the camp. The creek is far enough away from the road you shouldn't run into him, and the creek should cover your noise."

"Okay," Thomas said, not taking his eyes off the clearing.

Charlie held out his hand. "Give me the gun, Thomas. You don't want to shoot a boy."

Thomas looked grim when he handed Charlie back his .38.

Charlie knew Thomas wouldn't wait five minutes. He would be on his way as soon as his back was turned. He started around the knob at a dogtrot for the truck. He kept to what timber there was and tried not to make too much noise. As he opened the truck door, he paused and listened for a moment, thinking he heard shouting in the distance.

~~~~~~~

Thomas was more cautious than Charlie could have hoped, slinking down the hill like a cougar and into the little grove of black timber by the creek. The children were engrossed in their play and had moved even farther away from the cabin. The older girl, watching them from a distance, had a shoe off examining her foot. She didn't even look up when Thomas broke from the woods and ran to the children, whose backs were turned to him. Things were going well, he thought. He swooped Ida up from behind and gave her a big smile when she turned, surprised. He whirled for the creek just as a screech came from behind, and the older girl sprinted toward him with a vengeance. She was a hefty girl, and Thomas was amazed how fast she could move. The smaller children scattered like quail and took cover without a single sound. They didn't cry and carry on as some children might have done. They hid, he thought, much as they would during an enemy raid in olden times. It was a reflex action embedded in the most primitive cortex of their minds.

Thomas hit the creek full tilt, and his feet seemed almost not to touch the water as he splashed across.

The big girl, with a snarl on her lips and what Thomas thought must be the *Ute* war cry in her throat, came crashing on behind him. She appeared absolutely fearless, like a mother bear. The girl paid no heed to what she might be up against. She wore only one shoe, and when she hit the creek, she went down on the slick rocks but was back up almost instantly, determined as ever.

It will not go well for that girl if she catches up, Thomas thought. Even a girl that size should not be hard to fend off, but it might cost him some time. He didn't have time to waste on this wild girl. The two older women ran to the aid of the younger now, their screams urging her on. One of the women waved an axe.

Old trappers often said they would rather be captured by *Ute* warriors than by their women. The warriors would generally just kill you, they said.

Thomas knew, as he started up out of the creek bottom, he was losing ground. It wasn't like he had been working out or even running to meet the dawn each day.

He clawed at the saplings and chokecherries with one hand, holding on to Ida with the other as he half pulled his way up through the brush. Just as he shoved Ida up on top of the bank, he felt a strong hand on his ankle and saw the wide, dark face of the *Ute* girl twisted in a triumphant sneer. The screams from the two older women obviously bolstered the girl's courage, and she intended to acquit herself well. With Ida safe on the bank, Thomas turned and smiled at the girl before kicking her in the face with his heavy boot. This was not a game; she was lucky Charlie had the gun.

When Thomas pulled himself on up and grabbed the wide-eyed child back into his arms, he could hear the roar of the truck engine in the distance. He guessed if he angled slightly downslope after cresting the creek bank, he should hit the switchback just about right.

Charlie grinned at Ida when Thomas pushed her up into the cab of the truck. "Hi, Ida. How are you today?" The girl looked astounded.

"Grab some gears, my man," Thomas yelled breathlessly. "There's a war party of *Ute* women right behind me!" Thomas was high on victory, a rare thing for him, and he laughed as he turned to look out the back window. He guessed there would be a great wailing in the lodges of these *Ute* tonight. But someday they would sing songs about a young *Ute* girl who was fearless—like a mother grizzly.

7

The Sniper

Hiram Buck grew more consumed with worry each time his nephew reported back empty handed. On the third day he received word from the Uinta that Sally's daughter Ida Begay was stolen away. This was the final straw.

Hiram went into a temper, the likes of which had never been witnessed, even by his closest relatives. He knew now where the two Navajos had been.

He was wiped out. The sheriff's eviction notice was already tacked to his front door. This only added to the devastating news from his *Ute* relatives. Like an avalanche, everything was coming down on him at once. At last the big man fell into that cold, quiet fury feared most by those who knew him. It was out of his hands now. He was no longer in control of his own life.

Later that afternoon as Hiram sat on George Jim's rickety front porch, a .30-06 rifle across his lap, two dogs came passing through the property, as they often did after a day of carousing. One of the dogs belonged to George Jim but had taken to hanging out with the neighbor's dog when George Jim was away.

Hiram shot them both dead.

He was waiting for his nephew to come back, certain he would tell of yet another failure to find Charlie Yazzie; he intended to kill George Jim too.

~~~~~~

George Jim had twice before in early morning crept up the ridge above Aida Winters' place only to be disappointed each time to find the Navajo's truck still missing.

Now, for the third time, he bellied up through the grass on the ridge above the ranch. Still no Navajos. The only thing different this morning—Aida's truck was gone as well. He remembered then, it was sale day. Aida never missed a livestock sale if she could help it, especially not a horse sale.

Everything, at first, seemed quietly in order, but as he focused his attention on the house, he twice saw, within a matter of minutes, what he thought was the flick of a curtain in the front window. He put his scope on it and waited.

The sun came up fast, and it grew hot there in the grass at the top of the ridge. George just lay there, not moving a muscle, not even to bat a fly that was diligently working the corner of his left eye. Waiting was something he became very good at as a sniper. Waiting was what a sniper did mostly. The Army thought him quite talented in this regard and endeavored to develop those talents as best they could. Fortunately, he was somewhat genetically predisposed to it. Ninety percent of hunting is waiting, and hunting is what the *Ute* have always done best.

There it was again!

Someone was occasionally peeking out of those curtains. He was sure of it now but couldn't imagine who it might be. It was someone wanting to remain hidden but growing restless, tired of hiding. He saw this in big game. They would stay concealed, testing the air, examining the terrain, until they could stand it no more, and then they would simply appear as though they had worried the thing to death and nothing more could be done about it.

He could wait.

It was nearly an hour later when he watched the door open a nearly imperceptible crack. The buzz of a fly at his ear had almost lulled him into dozing. He would never have dozed off in the military, but here, he almost dozed off.

Eventually, the door opened a bit wider until he could just discern the outline of a face through his riflescope—a small face, that of a small person. She raised her face to the rising sun. It was a woman, and it seemed she had been missing the sun. But it wasn't until she cautiously edged out onto the porch with her arms outstretched that he could see who it was: Sally Klee.

George Jim nearly laughed aloud then. Suddenly, it was all so clear. What fools they had been. Aida Winters had been Sally's refuge when she was small, but no one paid attention to Sally Klee back then. Uncle Hiram would have a good laugh when he heard where she had been hiding all this time. So close to home. He would be proud of George Jim for working this out. They had been so certain she was somewhere in Farmington or maybe even Albuquerque, though God knows how she would have managed in so large a city.

He studied Sally more closely as she ventured to the edge of the porch, and then realizing the crosshairs were still centered on her, he moved them over a bit. The safety was off, and he had no real intention of squeezing the trigger.

It occurred to him this might have been his woman had his Aunt Tilde had her way. She had thought Sally the perfect match—one of the few girls in the area not so closely related; possibly only a distant cousin on the *Ute* side. If only Sally had waited as his aunt had wanted. But no, Sally had run away to Farmington and a life only whispered about among the family. All this could have been avoided perhaps had she waited. Perhaps he and Sally would be living in his little trailer together now, and those two children of hers would be his son and daughter, rather than that of the Navajo Thomas Begay.

Sally had her hair tied back, tied with one of Aida's long blue ribbons. She looked fresh and clean there on the porch, even pretty to George's way of thinking. He wondered if all that talk had been wrong. Maybe people had been wrong about Sally Klee. In his heart, however, he knew they weren't wrong.

Sally was moving about the porch now, enjoying the sun. She watched the horses for a moment then scanned the road and then the ridge. George Jim held his breath. Not a twitch or blink of an eyelid gave him away.

She turned once again to the horses. Her lips were moving, and though he could not hear the words at this distance, he thought she might be singing a little song, just as he remembered her doing when they were children. There had been a happy song about a pony. He thought maybe that was what she was singing.

The one-hundred-thirty grain boat-tail caught Sally just at the point of the breastbone, the velocity of the round so fast she felt no more than a bump—as though she had been lightly bumped on the chest by an open palm. She started forward, caught herself, and then sat heavily, flat on the porch. She raised her eyes to the sun, and the last image her brain received was of that brilliant orb—that great giver of life.

Through force of habit, George Jim's first move was to eject the empty and jack in a new round. He knew he wouldn't need a second shot, but this is the way he had been programmed. It cost nothing to be ready. He rose to one knee and picked up the spent brass, depositing it in his shirt pocket. He had often made a similar shot in the service, ending someone's life. It never bothered him then, no more than a deer or an elk would have. But this was different. Oh, he had shot women before and even children when it was determined they might have explosives strapped to them. He had not, however, shot a woman that might have one day become the mother of his children. It caught in his throat just then. He looked down at his two hands and, for just a moment, wished things might have been otherwise.

George Jim did not bother going down to the house. He felt no need to see that. He pulled a young sage and used it to brush out his sign there on the ridge and for a good piece down the trail as well. It really didn't matter. There would be someone along who knew how to track him. Eventually, they would come and try to kill him. He had already decided he would not allow them to take him to jail.

Maybe this would finally satisfy his Uncle Hiram; maybe he would get some money from this, and it would give him some breathing space. All Hiram needed was a little time.

He labored down off the ridge, not caring if he could be seen or not, coming eventually to the patch of oak brush leading down to his place. From a small open space, he could make out Hiram sitting on his front porch with something in his lap. At last he would have some good news for his uncle. Maybe Hiram could help him somehow with what he knew was coming.

As he broke through the brush at the edge of the clearing, he raised an arm in greeting, shouting to his uncle about who he had found. That's when the two dogs lying dead only a few feet apart caught his attention.

He instantly jerked his eyes to the distant porch. His uncle paid no heed to George Jim's shouting and even now was raising his rifle. He did not hesitate.

Hiram favored a heavier slug in a .30-06 and the two-hundred-twenty grain bullet boomed off the porch almost slow enough to be seen, should a person have the right angle on it. He was not the marksman George Jim was, but he could do a workmanlike job when he set his mind to it.

The bullet hit George Jim low in the belly with a *whomp*. There is no mistaking the sound of a large caliber rifle bullet in a gut shot. It took George Jim to his knees. His features registered surprise, and his big, wide face went slack. Instinctively, his own rifle came up, and he returned fire with that deadly accuracy born of gut-wrenching determination. The lighter .270 round hit Hiram just over the heart, but his greater body mass caused the hollow-point to mushroom with terrible effect. Both men, now mortally wounded, looked across the clearing at one another, and both grinned, a grin of satisfaction, each knowing they had finally shed themselves of a great burden.

George Jim, still on his knees, reloaded automatically without being aware of it.

Hiram was the luckier of the two as his wound was quickly fatal. The grin faded as he pitched forward out of his chair.

George Jim had seen countless gut-shot game—and people too. He knew this was going to take awhile. The big soft-nosed slug had plowed through his midsection, and while it had encountered virtually no other vital organ than his gut, it was a lethal wound.

George Jim thought it unfair that he should be the one to linger on in pain and suffering while his uncle, who was much more deserving in his opinion, was already wherever he was going to be. He raised his head slightly to look over at his dog. It had been gut-shot too but had lasted only a moment. The hydraulic shock alone probably brought near instant death. That had been his dog since it was a pup, and his Uncle Hiram knew how much store he sat by it.

That's why he killed it. Well, no matter. The score was even now.

What George really wanted was a drink of water. His mouth was dirt-dry, his belly on fire, intestines writhing with the peristaltic action that spewed their contents down his front and into the dirt of the yard. In olden times a gut shot was the easiest and most certain shot of all—always fatal in the end. It was a favorite target of the vengeful warrior—one who wanted an enemy's death to take a while. It was much the same, no matter what the weapon: knife, spear, arrow, or bullet. Nowadays, medical science might sometimes save a gut-shot person should help arrive in time, but even then that person would never be quite the same. Some, wounded in a like manner, may choose their own way out should means be available. It is those without means who are to be pitied.

Between excruciating spasms of pain, George Jim pulled the muzzle up tight under his chin.

~~~~~~~

On the way back from the Uinta, Charlie again stopped in Monticello for fuel. Leaving Thomas and Ida asleep in the truck, he went inside to call Aida and let her know they had the girl. There was no answer. He left the message on the machine, thanking her for her help and let her know they thought it best to get Ida back to Thomas's and her brother. He said they would be back for their horses as soon as possible.

He thought of calling Sue but didn't want to wake her ailing parents. He felt they would be back soon enough anyway. He went in the store and bought two coffees and a carton of milk. He also picked up a box of Thomas's favorite chocolate donuts. When he came out of the store, he saw Thomas just getting out of the truck.

"Aha!" was all Thomas said when he saw what Charlie had in his hand. He got back in the truck and turned to Ida. "I think Charlie has something you are really going to like!" he said.

It was quite late when they arrived in Shiprock, and Charlie could barely keep his eyes open. The adventures of the day had nearly worn Thomas and Ida to a frazzle as well. It was decided to pull into Charlie's place until daylight.

Ida took to Thomas immediately and soon made it known she

was starving. Nothing was open at that hour, and Charlie hoped he had enough food on hand to feed them.

Walking into the apartment, he immediately noticed the message light flashing on his phone. While Thomas and Ida rummaged through the refrigerator, Charlie picked up the receiver to hear his messages in private. He thought Sue may have left him something of a personal nature. Sue did leave several messages, including one saying Thomas's Uncle John Nez had arrived to help Lucy and her father. There were various other things from work—one from Pete Fish so garbled and rambling he couldn't make it out.

The last message was from Aida. In a strained but emotionless voice she told him about Sally Klee. She went on to tell him about the carnage authorities discovered at George Jim's place as well. She said they should not worry about the horses. She would care for them. At the end of the message, there was a catch in her voice as she let him know how happy she was they had found Ida. "Her middle name is Marie," she said, "like mine."

Charlie was stunned by the news and apparently it showed. As he hung up he saw Thomas looking at him in dismay.

"What, now?" Thomas mouthed over Ida's head. She was happily munching some crackers and cheese and paid no attention to the men as they moved to the living room.

At the whispered news, Thomas sat down heavily on the couch and took his head in his hands. Charlie touched his shoulder but could find no words he thought might help.

They made a bed for the girl on the couch, and Thomas arranged himself in the recliner with a blanket. Charlie lay down in his room, but only Ida really slept.

Thomas was up early and made coffee. He could hear Charlie taking a shower. As he sat at the kitchen table, the phone rang and he answered it. It was Sue calling from work. Charlie left a quick reply to her last message on her office line, telling her, among other things, he was back and they had Ida. Although it was her day off, she'd had a feeling he might call and went in early to check. Thomas told her about finding Ida and then about Sally but only the highlights as he thought it best she talk to Charlie when he was out of the shower.

They chatted for a minute, and again Sue made sure he knew his

Uncle John Nez was down from Navajo Mountain and staying out at Lucy's place. She mentioned Marissa being there as well in case Charlie had forgotten to tell him. Finally, she said she would meet them at the Dinè Bikeyah Café within the hour. They could all go out to his place together. Thomas thought this a good idea as he felt he and Lucy might need all the support they could get when they told the children their mother was gone. Marissa was there of course, but he thought it would be good if Sue was there too.

For a change, Charlie and his gang of two beat Sue to the cafe and had already ordered. Her favorite cinnamon bun was waiting when she arrived. After greeting everyone and giving Charlie a big hug, she was introduced to Ida.

Sue kneeled beside Ida's chair and talked to her at eye level. She told her what a pretty girl she was and how happy she was to meet her. She assured her that after breakfast they would see her brother Caleb. He missed her very much, she said, and couldn't wait to see her again.

This made Ida smile, and she began her breakfast with an appetite. Though they tried not to let it show, the adults fell under a pall even the bright and laughing young girl could not dispel.

After breakfast, everyone piled into Charlie's truck. There was room inside for everyone in these new trucks. In the old days the women and children rode bundled up in the open bed of the truck while the men were seated in the heated cab. This may have evolved from those long ago days when warriors stayed in the forefront. No one really knew why, but it had always been so. Just as the *hogan* belonged to the woman, the truck usually belonged to the man, just as the horses once had. Now, in a more enlightened age, women ride where they please, and men often ride space available. Some thought the new extended cab pickups may have had something to do with this.

They pulled up in the yard just as Caleb and old Paul T'Sosi were throwing a little of their precious hay to the ewes. The pregnant ewes had done well enough on the sparse pasture of spring, but now that they were nursing, they needed a little extra. The spring rains had not been generous.

Caleb spotted Charlie's truck and came running, shouting out loud when he saw Thomas and Ida in the front seat.

"Yaa' eh t'eeh," he exclaimed in his newly acquired Navajo accent, jumping up and down in his excitement. Thomas held open the door for his daughter, and she jumped down and ran to her brother, swinging him around in a hug and talking a steady stream of mixed *Ute* and English. The boy bobbed his head up and down and answered her questions in the same rapid-fire dialect.

Thomas smiled and watched the two of them then sent them off to the corrals where the old man waved but continued feeding his sheep. If he had not, the greedy ones would have got it all. The lambs and kids were milling around the outside of the small band, waiting their chance. Ida clapped her hands at the sight. It had been a long time since she had seen kids and lambs.

Thomas's Uncle John Nez and Marissa came from the summer *hogan* followed by Lucy, who had been showing Marissa how the loom was set up for the day's weaving. Today she would begin the new weaving for the trader, and Marissa didn't want to miss a single step. The adults gathered in a circle, and Charlie informed the family of all that had happened up in Ute country, and finally, the news of the recent death of Sally Klee.

When he was finished, Thomas looked at Lucy and pointed to the shorthaired young girl in coveralls at the corrals. "Her name is Ida Marie, and she will live with us now…if you will have it."

Lucy just nodded as though there had never been any question and went to make coffee for everyone. She met her father on his way up from the corrals, and they smiled silently at one another and nodded in passing.

After being introduced to Ida Marie, everyone sat in the cool shade of the brush arbor thinking about this girl who spoke broken Navajo. Ida stood quietly with her head up during the introductions, and everyone later said she presented herself well. Her mother taught her some manners, they thought, and though she had not been to school, she appeared very bright and, unlike Caleb, was also very outgoing. They all agreed it would not be long before she caught up to her classmates. Marissa said she would be glad to tutor her while they were there.

"I taught school part-time when I was getting my masters," she said quietly. "I think we can get her up to speed in no time."

Sue pitched in too. "I can help out on weekends." She laughed and told Lucy, "It looks like you and I will be making another trip to the mall."

"That will be good," Lucy's father noted. "I still want to see about getting Caleb those boots."

Ida Marie once again ran off with Caleb, this time to see what he had taught the dog. The dog met them with a knowing grin.

With their full coffee cups sitting on the old trestle table, everyone seemed deep in thought regarding how many things would have to be done now that the children were part of the family.

Thomas and Lucy had finally decided they would wait until they were alone with the children before telling them about their mother. Both dreaded the very thought of it.

~~~~~~~

The next morning Charlie called the Coroner's office in Cortez and had him forward a copy of Sally Klee's death certificate to him at legal services. He promised Thomas he would also immediately start work on custody papers for the children.

His next call was to Aida Winters. He found her reserved but friendly and willing to keep their horses until they could come for them.

"Charlie, when you and Thomas come for the horses, I would appreciate it if you could bring Sally's children so I can at least see them." She hesitated briefly as though thinking about something. "I intend to purchase Hiram Buck's property from the bank next month. It's been run into the ground as you know—overgrazed, eroded, and the buildings fit only to be bulldozed." Her voice grew more determined. None of the Buck clan can come up with the money to redeem it, and I doubt anyone else around here will want it either, considering what's happened and its condition."

Charlie was confused. "It will be years before it's recovered enough to be of any value, and that's only if no stock is kept on it. Why would you want it, Aida?"

"I don't want it," Aida said abruptly, "but someday it will be worth something...enough to give those children a start."

Charlie hadn't realized how close Aida and Sally had been.

"I'll talk to Thomas about bringing the children. I'm sure that won't be a problem."

Aida went on, "I know how Navajo feel about the dead, Charlie, so I'm having Sally buried here on my place." Her voice became firm. "She and Thomas were never married, and she had no other close relatives that gave a damn about her. If Thomas has a problem with this have him give me a call."

Charlie assured her he would speak to Thomas and, before hanging up, again thanked her for keeping the horses.

Sue dropped by his desk to confirm their lunch plans.

"So, you finally got yourself a horse, huh?" She did not say this in an accusatory manner. In fact, Charlie thought she actually seemed pleased.

Lucy told her about the horses, in private, the day before. "A man who has a horse will soon need a place to keep it," Lucy had said. That little place in the country seemed closer than ever, and Sue smiled at the thought.

"Uh…well, yeah, I had a chance to buy that gelding I used to go get Caleb." He fidgeted. "At the price, I couldn't pass him up."

"Well, now you and Thomas have horses, and Lucy can use her dad's old horse, so I guess you better keep an eye out for one for me," she said as she dropped the mail on his desk. She turned and left before he could say anything.

Later at the Dinè Bikeyah, Charlie ordered the Navajo taco platter. He had been craving one since the cafe in Bluff. He shouldn't have let that ill-natured *Ute* girl sway him. He looked over at Sue's chef's salad and was glad he had gone for something more substantial. Rabbit food, who could live on that?

"Where was Pete Fish this morning?" he asked, mostly just in the way of conversation.

"He hasn't been in the last few days. Word has it he's working on a big project for some of the councilmen."

Charlie had a big bite of fry-bread halfway to his mouth but put his fork down and looked thoughtful. "Which councilmen?" he asked.

"No one knows for sure. It's something he says is pretty hush-hush; I don't see any files on it coming from the secretarial pool. He usually has me look his stuff over for errors, but not lately."

"Have you had a chance to get that list of indictments in the Greyhorse case that we talked about last week?"

"Yes, I did. I put a manila folder marked GREYHORSE IN-DICTMENTS in your in-box." Sue sounded a little exasperated at the question. "What's up?"

"I'm not sure really. Just a few little things that don't add up. They've been running through my mind lately, and they all seem to go back to Pete Fish." He looked Sue directly in the eye. "How's he been acting?"

She knew what he meant and tried to make as little of it as possible. "Same as always, I guess." she looked down at her salad. "He asked me out again last week...for the third time." She hesitated and decided to tell him. "When I turned him down, told him I didn't think you'd like it, he said something a little strange."

Charlie straightened. "And what might that be?"

"He said I'd better reconsider my options; you might not be around forever!"

"Really! Did he happen to say why?" Charlie's lips were smiling, but his eyes weren't.

"Nope, and I didn't feel like chasing after him to find out why either. That guy's a nut-job, boss or no boss."

"The guy's got a screw loose, all right. He's been obsessed with you from the start. I don't like the turn this is taking. I'm pretty sure he's hiding something!"

"He came out clean in the conspiracy investigation. No one could link him to the corruption or murders." Sue said this without conviction and Charlie nodded. He felt much the same himself.

"There's more to it than we know. I'm more and more convinced Pete's involved in this, one way or another."

The waitress brought their check, momentarily interrupting the conversation.

Charlie brightened considerably. "Hey, there's a little place down by Waterflow that just came on the market. The house is nothing special, but it could be with a little work. Only five acres, but it's got some trees and some irrigation." He glanced up at the ceiling. "I thought maybe we could take a little run out there after work and look it over?"

102

8

The Meeting

Pete Fish was more than a little nervous about meeting with the two council members. He really had no need to be, as far as he knew. Still, he had to admit only blind, stumbling luck had intervened in his favor. The important thing was he was back in the good graces of his new employers—people who held a great personal interest in witnesses in the ongoing Greyhorse murder and corruption proceedings. Only months now separated them from their possible trial date, should further indictments be forthcoming. This made them anxious to eliminate as many variables as possible. As he pulled into the parking lot at the Holiday Inn, he went over in his mind what he planned to say.

Room 202 was a corner suite overlooking the parking lot. It seemed to him a wasted expense for the purpose, but money seemed no object with these people, as he well knew. He parked at the side of the building on the far side of the dumpsters.

They told him precisely when to be there, and Pete was exactly on time. He hoped punctuality was important. He entered the hotel through a side door as instructed then took the stairs. He knocked softly on the door. There was a pause, and he assumed someone was looking through the peephole—that's what he would have done.

A tall, thin, sinister-looking man, whose hair was put up on the back of his neck in the old way, finally opened the door. He seemed somewhat young for a council member. This must be the notorious Robert Ashki of whom he had heard so much. The man did not speak but ushered him into the room with something akin to a flourish.

The other man in the room was sitting. Pete Fish recognized him instantly from his photo in the weekly Navajo newspaper. Donald Benally was first to speak. A man in his early fifty's, he wielded an inordinate amount of power on the reservation. He was a small man with close-cropped graying hair and a paunch. He had, so far, remained unscathed in the scandal following the arrests.

"Ah, Fish, good to meet you!" he said coming forward and taking Pete's hand. "We are, so far, quite pleased with your handling of…uh, your little project." He frowned momentarily. "It appeared things might be off track for a while, but now, with the recent happenings in Colorado, we are beginning to see a little daylight. The matter now appears resolvable."

Robert Ashki, also not named in the indictments, did not introduce himself but rather interrupted the smaller man somewhat rudely, Pete Fish thought.

"The big question is what is being done about the remaining two witnesses?" The thin man was a member of the populous Salt People Clan near Rainbow Bridge. Twice elected by his constituency, he held sway over a healthy majority in his part of the country.

Pete Fish cleared his throat and worded his reply as carefully as possible.

"Gentlemen, as Mr. Benally mentioned, not only has one problem been eliminated, but it has been accomplished at virtually no expense to yourselves, other than my own rather small consulting fee." He smiled benignly at the pair. "There was a healthy amount of funds allocated to that problem. I am happy to say it may now be reassigned to a larger and more pressing purpose."

"Yazzie and Begay, you mean?" The rough-mannered Robert Ashki liked plain talk, and this flowery beating around the bush did not impress him in the least. Unlike them he had not gone to a university and held that thinly veiled disdain for higher learning so prevalent among those who have pulled themselves up by their bootstraps.

Pete Fish tried not to let the provincial councilman's remark anger him. The man's reputation was well known. This was no time to let even the slightest dissension mar his meticulously thought out presentation.

"Exactly," Pete agreed in as curt a manner as he dared. "I believe we can resolve the entire issue within days, with a little luck."

Donald Benally beamed at this and turned to his fellow councilman. "Did you hear that, Robert? 'Within days,' the man said!" He nodded agreeably to Robert Ashki.

"What I heard was, 'with luck.' I prefer not to risk the rest of my life on 'Luck!'" He raked Pete Fish with a cold stare. "My sources tell me your little success last week was more than luck."

Pete Fish smiled, prematurely, as it turned out.

"No!" Ashki went on, "it was more on the order of a miracle! They seem to think you recruited idiots. They could have cost us a great deal, and I'm not talking about money."

Donald Benally was somewhat taken aback at this talk and looked immediately to Pete Fish for some sort of denial.

"Those people came well recommended...and I might add, by one of your fellow council members—the one you sent with the money, though I understand he is now in jail awaiting bond." Pete Fish had hoped the talk would go smoother than this. The Grand Jury recently made it known there were secret indictments still in the offing. No one knew who would be next. These people were clearly frightened, and he wondered for a moment if he too might be in more danger than he previously thought.

"I want to make this very plain to you, Fish! The people you have dealt with in the past are no longer key. You are dealing with us now, and I'm telling you plain and simple, should you fail in this, there will be serious consequences." Robert Ashki had done his own due diligence and was not to be swayed in the matter.

"You told us Yazzie couldn't be bought." Ashki's eyes glittered. "Did you even try?"

Donald Benally also looked at Pete, the question obvious in his eyes.

Pete Fish recoiled mentally but desperately hoped it did not show. "I'm telling you both right now! Charlie Yazzie cannot be bought. The other maybe, but not Yazzie." Pete had gone over and over this in the past. They apparently thought everyone was as corrupt as they were. "Charlie Yazzie will have to be killed to keep him out of that courtroom!" There, Pete Fish had made it as plain as possible.

"Do you want us to bring in outside help?" Benally could not imagine an outsider being able to make this thing happen, but he thought to spur Pete Fish to some sort of extra effort.

Robert Ashki spoke almost in a whisper. "There are people in Albuquerque who can take care of this, if you can't." And then louder, "We are running out of time! Let us know soon, should you decide you need help."

Donald Benally looked surprised and, for just a moment, as though he might want to interject something further but thought better of it and just shook his head.

Robert Ashki stood and prepared to leave, motioning for his fellow councilman to follow. He cautioned Pete Fish. "Wait a few minutes before leaving and, again, go out by the side entrance."

After the councilmen closed the door behind them, Pete Fish immediately went to the suite's refrigerator and, with trembling hands, made himself a stiff drink, using two of the little bottles of bourbon.

At the window he watched the black Suburban drive out of the parking lot and hoisted his drink at the departing car. He thoughtfully fingered his turquoise ring. It had been his father's ring. Pete felt it brought him luck, though it certainly hadn't done so for his father.

Pete Fish had good enough reason to want Charlie Yazzie dead, and money had nothing to do with it. It was time to put up or shut up, he figured. The time for intermediaries or outside help was past. He would fix this thing once and for all. There might be great rewards in the offing, should this go right.

~~~~~~~

Aida Winters had Sally Klee buried on a little rise just up from the house at ten a.m. on a clear, sunny morning. Aida's husband was already buried there in a plot right next to the one she had marked out for herself. There was just room for Sally between them. Her husband had not known Sally, but he was a kind man who loved children, even though he had none of his own. Aida felt sure he would not mind Sally being there.

Some men she hired from town dug the grave by hand so as not to disturb the other two plots. They said they would return the following morning for the burial and fill in the grave. The next morning, when the funeral director brought Sally home, Aida had the plain pine box placed on a small wagon. She and Sally had used that wagon in the garden when Sally was small. Aida hitched her own horse to it for the short pull up the hill. She led the horse herself, and the funeral director brought up the rear, carrying two small sprays of flowers, one from Charlie and Sue and one from Thomas and the children. Sue had made the arrangements, and the flowers were just as she had ordered. Aida would bring her own flowers later from her and Sally's garden. There would be no headstone, just as there was none for her husband, and there would be none for her. This would be the end of the line for them all, literally. Navajos do not often come looking for the graves of their people, and she and her husband had none left to look for theirs.

The gravediggers arrived during the short reading from the Bible and stood quietly to the side. The funeral director thought the reading part of his job. Aida was not a religious person and knew Sally had not been either, but there seemed to be something right about it there on that sunny, blue-skied morning, and she let him perform the small ceremony as he thought proper.

After Aida threw in the first handful of dirt, she stood back waiting for the men to fill the grave. It occurred to her then she had neglected to tell Thomas something. Sally mentioned it only days before she died. Something she said Thomas might want to know. It was probably not even important now after all that had happened, but she would try to remember it and let Thomas know when he came for the horses.

Later that evening, when she was alone, she thought back to all Sally Klee had told her. How there were many forces at work to insure her silence and that of Thomas Begay and Charlie Yazzie. She told Aida those powerful people would kill them all if they could. They were big people with big money, she said. One way or the other they would get everyone on their list. That's why she had decided to take the money, she said. Not only might it save her life, but more importantly, it could save the lives of her children.

When Aida first asked who her contact was, Sally said she forgot his name. She later admitted it was Councilman Robert Ashki.

She said he told her if she ever revealed him to anyone, she would be sorry, then threatened her with atrocities beyond the imagining of a white woman.

Now Sally was gone.

Aida would make them all sorry for that. In the morning she would call up this Robert Ashki, mention Sally Klee's name. He would be more than willing to meet with her when she was through telling him what she knew.

She would bring the wrath of God down on these people. If indeed there was a God.

9

The Gathering

Thomas and Lucy agreed it would be a good thing to hold a little gathering to welcome their new children to the family and perhaps help draw them closer. It would be good, they thought, if the children could become acquainted with some of the other children in the area before school started. First, however, Ida Marie would need proper clothes and perhaps a little something special for the party.

Once again, Sue Hanagarni agreed to meet them at the mall to help pick out school supplies and clothes for Ida Marie. Lucy told Thomas, "Sue has been around town kids more. She has a better idea of what the latest thing might be. It's important for a young girl to present herself well on her first day of school."

Marissa and John originally planned to come along to the mall as well but, at the last minute, decided to stay so Marissa could catch up on her writing. John agreed to take the sheep out, though he was not much on sheep anymore since he had become a cattleman. No one felt the children were in any particular danger now, and Lucy's father would be along to help in any case.

At the mall the old man took Caleb with him to look at those nice boots he picked out for the boy on their last visit. Caleb had never worn any shoes other than sneakers. Now it was time for man shoes: boots. The old man was almost as excited as the boy, and they laughed as Caleb stomped around the store in the boots.

They bought them slightly too large so he could "grow" into them. They might last him six months fitted this way if he doesn't wear them out doing what boys always do, Paul thought.

"Those boots are a good brand and will last a long time," he told Caleb, "if you will just stay out of the water and put a little mutton tallow on them from time to time."

The boy eagerly agreed to this, though secretly Paul knew if he was like most little boys, he will forget to do either of these things.

At the end of the day, the family had run through nearly all the cash they held in reserve. Thomas did hold back the money he owed Charlie on the horse, but that was it. They were satisfied with their purchases and felt well prepared for their first school year.

~~~~~~~

Paul T'Sosi killed a kid goat and a lamb for the get together his daughter planned. It would be just friends and family, but Paul knew there was no telling how many would show up. He didn't want anyone going away hungry. That would be embarrassing. If there were any leftovers, the people would wrap them up and take them with them. It would be considered rude to do otherwise.

Thomas's Uncle John Nez told Paul about a good way to cook underground. "They did wild pigs this way over there," he said, referring to his time in the service. "It makes my mouth water to think of it. You dig a trench about three or four feet deep and line it with rocks. Then you build a big fire in it until it goes to coals and the rocks turn white hot." He paused here to lick his lips. "Then lay down a layer of damp earth over the stones—about a foot."

He had the old man's attention.

"In the islands they used banana leaves over damp earth to cover the hot stones. They wrapped the meat in banana leaves too. Up at our place we put a layer of earth down on the rocks and then a sheet of rusted roofing tin. You can use an old pounded-out car fender or trunk lid too." John Nez looked at the old man. "Just make sure all the galvanizing or paint is burned off." He stopped to think; he wanted everything to be exactly in order.

"Then season the meat how you like it. You can slather it in barbeque sauce or just add chopped garlic and salt and pepper...or ground red chilies." He was smiling now, remembering the islands. "Wrap the quarters in clean flour sacks and then put each piece in several wet gunny sacks tied up with bailing wire. Wet them down sopping wet so they don't scorch. He was getting into it now, moving his hands to show how it was all done. "Place the wrapped meat on the first layer of tin and cover it with another piece of tin. Now you put down an extra-heavy layer of damp earth—at least sixteen inches—over everything. Build another big fire on top." John Nez was embellishing the instructions with elaborate hand gestures now, showing exactly how the earth was spread around and the top fire kept burning evenly over the pit.

"That fire has to keep going for at least six or eight hours," he cautioned. "Let the fire die down then for a few hours. Then uncover the meat and carefully unwrap it. It will be falling off the bone!" He smacked his lips. "It's delicious! The best you ever put your tongue to."

Paul T'Sosi was sold and anxious to try this. "We've got plenty of old rusted tin!" he asserted. He had always prided himself on his outdoor cooking.

"It's a lot of work but it's worth it. Once you try it you'll know why. People will talk about it for a long time," John assured him.

Paul had listened intently. He had an excellent memory for an old man and seldom forgot anything he was told. He could see everything in his mind just as described. "I have heard of pit cooking, but I never seen it done before."

John nodded knowingly. "We may not have banana leaves out here, but what we do have is plenty of cedar wood. That cedar flavor is just the best to my way of thinking. Lots better than oak or apple wood like some use. The meat will melt in your mouth."

The old man was fascinated. They had always roasted goat and mutton the traditional way—grilled over the coals. That is, when they did not fry it up in a pot of oil that could then be used to do the fry-bread.

Stews were more popular back when he was a boy. You could feed a lot of people with a stew, and no one had to go away hungry.

The two men started digging the pit the very next morning. The children helped by gathering large stones and dragging up cedar wood picked from the winter supply behind the *hogan*. It was going to take a lot of wood, but Paul said he knew of an old, dead cedar tree down the wash. It should be plenty, he thought.

~~~~~~~

Charlie and Sue came out early the day of the party. They knew Lucy and the others would need all the help they could get. Though it was intended to be a family affair, word on the reservation gets around. Anyone who dropped by would be welcomed and fed accordingly. The men fashioned long tables, using borrowed sawhorses and timber planks, and set them up under the brush arbor. Navajos do not straggle in for such festivities. Latecomers would have to make do sitting on the old wagon bed or the flatbed of the Dodge truck. Pickup trucks would be backed up and tailgates let down for seating.

Word had gotten out, and Paul now expected a good deal more hungry guests than first thought. He was not really surprised. It was to be expected. The previous evening he decided to add an additional yearling lamb to the menu.

The fires were started well before daylight. By the time the sun was up, the meat was in the ground and the top fires burning. The men stood off from the blazing pit satisfied the meat would be done when the guests arrived.

Lucy, Sue, and Marissa had not been idle. Two five-gallon containers of pinto beans, slow-cooked with salt pork and red chili flakes, simmered on the stove. An iron caldron of oil stood ready on the grill outside to fry the massive amount of fry-bread dough Marissa was kneading on the kitchen table. Large tubs of sodas and bottled water were waiting for friends from town to bring ice on their way out. Lucy stood in the middle of the yard trying to think if they had forgotten anything. Many guests, she knew, would bring an additional dish or dessert to round out the meal.

Alcohol was not encouraged and not often a problem at these family gatherings, but there would still be the hidden bottle, secretly shared behind a pickup truck on the fringes. As long as this did not get out of hand, it was generally overlooked, and no great stigma was attached to those who behaved themselves.

By noon, vehicles began to arrive and more and more men gathered at the fire as they would have in any previous age. They talked of livestock and horses and, of course, the high price of feed. Pickup trucks were compared, and Charlie's new Chevy fell in for a good bit of discussion.

Children ran through the festivities "like wild Indians," in Thomas's words. Ida Marie and Caleb were right in the middle of them and just as loud as any their age.

Paul T'Sosi and several other older men gravitated to one side, discussing issues more aligned to their interest, remembering times gone by. A tall paper cup of peach schnapps was passed around, and Paul took a good swallow. He abhorred drunkenness but was not, himself, a teetotaler.

Charlie watched Sue help the women and girls who gathered to cover the serving table and lay out boxes of plastic tableware alongside stacks of paper plates. She was smiling and talking to people, some of whom she had not seen for years. On the reservation one might go a long time without seeing someone they had gone to school with or were even related to. The Dinè Bikeyah is a very large place and people there tend to spread out. They like "elbow room."

Paul, John, and Charlie finally uncovered the cooking pit. The coals had nearly died out and were easily shoveled aside by the men holding long poles with hay hooks wired to the ends. They now snagged the bundles out of the heat and quickly carried them up to the recently cleared table. "Stand back!" they called as they moved through the crowd with the poles. Children were pulled out of their way, and many exclaimed over the number of steaming packages. The wire wraps were cut away, and the sacking carefully cut and laid open. Immediately, the most delicious aroma filled the air. The smell caused people to look around hungrily and call the children.

Now Uncle John Nez, Charlie, and Thomas sliced great pans of tender lamb and kid goat and tried to calculate the number of arriving guests. They hoped they would not run short. Trucks and a few cars were parked nearly halfway out to the highway now. Thomas pointed out a brand new black Ford dually. It was the very expensive King Ranch model, considered rare in those parts.

"Anyone know who owns that black Ford?" Thomas asked.

Charlie studied the truck for a moment but shook his head. On the reservation, trucks were as individual as their owners and usually as easily recognized. "I've never seen it," he finally decided.

John Nez had not taken his eyes off the truck from the time it had pulled in. He surprised them both when he said, "Utah plates. I think I know who it is."

The other two men looked from him to the truck several times before Thomas spoke. "How's that, Uncle John?"

"That truck's from my county—Navajo Mountain area." He nodded as though to himself. "It's him alright."

Charlie squinted at the truck. "Who is it?"

"Robert Ashki. He's our councilman up at Navajo Mountain." He shook his head. "Now why would a councilman from that far away show up at this little party?"

The name did not ring a bell with Thomas, and Charlie thought it only vaguely familiar. Only twenty-four Tribal Council members represent the entire Navajo Reservation—an area encompassing portions of three states. Even so, the average Navajo knows but a few councilmen, generally only the ones from his area.

There had once been eighty-eight councilmen.

"That number had to be cut down," Thomas said, "because there was just not enough money to satisfy so many corrupt councilmen."

No one had gotten out of the Ford or even rolled down a window. Just as Thomas decided to walk down there, Paul T'Sosi began beating on a washtub, meaning dinner was ready to be served. People began queuing up for utensils, and as usual, the meat would be first on their plates. Children were cautioned to pipe down, stop running around kicking up dust, and to stay away from the boiling fry-bread pot. Charlie grabbed a pair of tongs and started dishing out lamb. Thomas and John Nez followed suit.

There was much laughter and quiet banter among the guests, and plates were piled high with succulent barbeque. Steam from the pans caused the servers to sweat. John Nez and Thomas thought to wear bandanas on their foreheads, but Charlie, unaccustomed to wearing a headband, had not remembered to bring one and constantly wiped his brow. There was a good reason Indians used to wear headbands, he realized. Occasionally, he glanced out the front of the shelter to the road and parked vehicles beyond. The black Ford was still there. Charlie noticed John Nez checking it out too.

They were nearly done serving the first round and beginning to see the second-helping people in line. Charlie looked up to see a tall man, with his hair up in a bun, standing in front of him with his plate held out. He was well dressed, wearing a black Stetson hat and turquoise bracelet with a matching belt buckle. He smiled thinly but did not speak. John Nez, on the other side of Thomas and partially hidden, suddenly put his hand out.

"You are far from home today, councilman." He said this in a pleasant but questioning manner. The councilman was taken aback to see someone who knew who he was. He had not figured on this, and his surprise was apparent.

"Well, hello John. I might say the same of you." He moved down the line in front of John without thanking Charlie for his helping of lamb. "I'll try a little of that goat if that is what you've got there."

"Yes, and you'll never taste better, councilman." The two men eyed one another. They had known each other many years, and each was well aware of the other's reputation. John gave him a healthy portion of kid and said, "Find a seat, Robert. I'll catch up with you when this line slows down."

Robert Ashki nodded but did not answer. He seemed more than a little put out by the chance meeting. He moved off across the crowded eating area and did not look back.

Without appearing rude, Charlie had paid as close attention to the talk between the two men as possible. He was close to the end of the serving table and not far from Sue, who was manning the bean pots.

"Sue," he hissed. And again, "Sue!" Finally, she turned from the steaming kettles red-faced but smiling.

"What?" she asked, arching an eyebrow. She was having a good time. It had been a while since she had done anything like this, and she was happy to be there among friends and neighbors.

Charlie whispered, "Do you remember a Councilman Robert Ashki on any of the paperwork you processed in the files of the

Greyhorse case?

Sue turned back to the pots and ladled another dipper of beans into a teenagers bowl. "Uh, I don't think so. Why do you ask?"

Charlie held up a finger. "We'll talk in a minute." He stabbed another forkful of lamb for an old woman who once worked for the tribal business office. She helped him with grant applications when he was at the university. She remembered him, laughed, and mentioned some small joke he had once played on her. Charlie did not remember doing that but, nonetheless, loaded her plate down with the better cuts of lamb. He knew she would take home what she didn't finish, and her forty-five-year-old son, who still lived with her, would have it for his supper. He was a heavy drinker and would surely have starved without her.

After nearly everyone had gone through the line a second time, getting plates of food to take home, Charlie was finally completely out of lamb. John and Thomas ran out of goat soon after. Everyone agreed it was as good a barbeque as they ever put in their mouth.

Fortunately, Lucy made sure large containers of everything had been put aside for the servers; no one would go hungry tonight.

Marissa was worn out from hours making fry-bread. The family was proud of the way she hung in there and never once asked for help. She spoke good enough Navajo that even the old people could mostly understand her. Those old ones thought it quite something for a white woman to speak Navajo so well. There were a few missionaries they could understand, and of course, what few old traders were left were fairly fluent, but none of those people were as good as they thought they were.

White people always had a hard time with the language, often because the Navajo would play jokes on them and tell them a certain thing was one thing, when really it was another—often something bawdy. The Navajo love a good joke and would later laugh among themselves when the white person repeated the phrase to someone who spoke the language. Usually that person would instantly catch on to the joke and run with it. In the old days many a winter's evening had been pleasantly whiled away at the local trading post "teaching" a new trader the language. It might be years before someone felt sorry enough for him to set things straight.

When John Nez was finally able to leave his post at the serving table, he went in search of Councilman Ashki. It was late afternoon now, and many guests were calling their children and packing up their vehicles. As John Nez moved through the crowd, he was recognized from the serving line and received many compliments on the food. He gave all the credit to Lucy and her old father, which was the right thing to do. Later, when his words got back to Paul T'Sosi, the old man smiled and thought even more of John Nez.

Councilman Ashki was nowhere to be found. Charlie and Thomas joined in, moving through the people and asking if anyone had seen the tall man with the good turquoise and black Stetson. Many noticed him but none saw him go. When the three got to the edge of the parking area, they could see the black truck was gone. After the crowd thinned, the three men walked down the road to where it had been parked. Two old men had their pickups parked nose to nose with the hoods up. The eldest was running jumper cables to the other's battery. Thomas recognized the man with the cables as a distant relative of Lucy's.

"*Shahastoi,*" he called to the elderly man whose name he could not remember. "Did you see the man in that fancy truck that was parked here?"

The old man reached in and clipped the battery cables on before answering. "I saw him…there was a woman in the truck too, but I couldn't see her very well. I don't know who they were. They were not from around here, I think." He looked down the road. "They had bad manners!"

"Why do you say that, Uncle?"

The old man pointed to a full plate of food that had been thrown across the ground where the black truck had been parked.

"That is a bad way to treat good food," and he turned back to the dead battery. "Those people must never been hungry."

He waved a hand in the air. "Try to start it now, *Atsilli!*" he called to his brother.

"There was a woman?" Charlie looked at John Nez. "Does he have a wife?"

"He is a big man in our part of the country. Yes, he has a wife, but there are any number of women it might have been."

Robert Ashki had, several times when John was away, come by the place to speak to Marissa. He told her he was available for interviews regarding tribal culture and government, should she have need of such information. Marissa had not responded favorably, and he finally stopped coming around.

When the guests had finally all gone, the party givers, worn now to the bone, settled themselves in the brush arbor, quietly enjoying the food Lucy had put back for them. Again Lucy and her father were commended for the success of the gathering. Paul T'Sosi and John Nez many times that day basked in the praise of the hungry people. The children became friends with many of their future classmates and should not feel out of place come the first day of school. Caleb and Ida Marie were now, once again, down at the corrals, trying to figure out which kids and lambs were left after the barbeque.

Marissa made one last batch of hot fry-bread just for them, and Lucy thought it nearly as good as her own. The oil had been much used by then. She allowed that may have taken a little away from it.

John Nez spoke across the table to Marissa. "Well then, did you see Councilman Ashki come through the line?"

"Councilman Ashki?" She registered surprise. "What would he be doing down here?" She paused then said, "I must have been pretty awful at work not to notice that fancy young man." She said this last in Navajo, and it had not come out exactly right, causing Lucy and her father to hide a smile.

"No one knows what he was doing down here. If it were up in our district, I would say he was out stumping for votes. He never misses a free feed up there. He has no supporters down here, though. Strange!"

Charlie spoke up. "I saw him looking over at Thomas before he even got in line. He must have asked around to find out who he was."

Thomas frowned. "I never saw him before in my life. I wouldn't have given him a second look if Uncle John hadn't spoken to him."

~~~~~~~

As Councilman Robert Ashki pulled his big truck back up on the highway, he turned to Aida Winters. "Are you sure you can go through with this?" he asked.

"Thomas Begay has it coming!" was all she said, reaching up and taking the binoculars off the dashboard and putting them away in the glove box.

"You're probably right....and too, this will allow us to leave the children out of it. With Thomas gone you may well get those kids—with my help."

His fellow council member Donald Benally may have thought that pompous ass Pete Fish could handle Charlie Yazzie, but he himself had his doubts. Pete Fish was too soft in his opinion. A big talker and that was all. They needed someone with grit for this job. He'd also had doubts when Aida first contacted him, but now, after this meeting, he was of a totally different mind. She might be exactly who they needed.

Aida looked over at him and said as though reading his thoughts, "When Sally told me you were the one who approached her, I first thought it might be a mistake getting in touch with you. But the more I thought about it, the more I figured there was a reckoning coming one way or the other. I knew Hiram Buck couldn't handle your problem."

Aida looked out the window at the great Shiprock in the distance. *Tse Bit'a'I*, "the Rock with Wings" the Navajo call it.

Robert Ashki followed Aida's gaze. "My people believe they were brought to this country on the back of that great winged rock."

"Well," Aida said, looking around, "it brought them to a hell of a place."

The councilman just smiled. He wasn't much on mythology himself. He checked his rearview mirror as though thinking they might be followed.

"Now that I know John Nez is Thomas's uncle, I have my doubts Thomas could ever have been bought off in the first place. John Nez is an idealistic fool. He and I have bumped heads many times over the years." He scowled. "Now, he listens too much to that white woman he has taken up with. I expect she'll have him running for my seat on the council next."

Aida eyed him with a calculating glance. He was not one to judge a white woman, she thought to herself and smiled.

10

The Surprise

Pete Fish arrived at the office early and was waiting when Charlie came in.

"I hear you people had a little party out at Thomas Begay's place," he said cheerfully. "I wish I could have made it, but I was out of town."

"Sorry you missed it," Charlie said, though it was all he could do to sound civil. "You haven't been around much the last week or so." He lifted his eyebrows. "Special project?"

"You might say that, I guess. Hush-hush council business, you know." He replied with a secretive smile."

"Um, well, Sue seems to be handling the office all right while you are gone."

"Yes, that girl is something special. It will be a lucky man that winds up with her!"

"Oh, I know. I was just telling her that the other night. We went to look at a little place together."

A cloud passed over Pete's face, and he had to look away for a moment.

"Well, I wouldn't be rushing into anything just yet."

"Really! Have you heard something I haven't?" Charlie grinned. "The old man's not going to fire me, is he?" he said, knowing full well he was the fair-haired boy of the moment in the front office.

"Uh, well no, I haven't heard anything." Pete said frowning. "I just meant…well, you know how it is—fate can just step in sometimes and usually when you least expect it." He shook his head. "No one is safe from the law of chance; just when you think things are going well, Boom! Everything changes." Pete Fish seemed a bit more cheerful after saying this. "The reason I came in early this morning was to catch you before you were out and about. I need some help on a little project I'm working on and thought you could lend a hand. It will require a little trip together. I've already asked the old man, and he's okay with it." He watched Charlie closely. "I was thinking we could take off first thing tomorrow morning."

Charlie could see this was more of an edict than a request. He nodded and walked over to greet Sue Hanagarni, who had just walked in.

Pete Fish followed him with an icy stare and then, not being able to watch the two of them together any longer, turned and left the office.

Charlie approached Sue, who even now had a questioning look on her face.

"What was that all about? You two looked pretty chummy."

"Yep, he and I are like this," he said, crossing one finger over the other and grinning. "In fact he's invited me on a little outing tomorrow morning."

"Oh? Where to?"

"He didn't say. His work is all very hush-hush, you know."

"Well, that doesn't sound good to me. I think there could be more to it."

Charlie grimaced. "You know, I think you might be right."

He and Sue went over the to-do list for the day. He hoped he could clean up some neglected paperwork before leaving with Pete Fish the next morning.

Charlie didn't think Pete Fish capable of violent behavior. They were, after all, fellow alumni, though Pete had graduated long before Charlie, and with both an accounting and law degree. He was still called the "bean counter" by some who thought him a little too meticulous in perusing their monthly expense accounts.

~~~~~~~

The following morning as Charlie drove to meet Pete Fish at the office, the added weight of the stainless .38 seemed to tug at the shoulder harness under his jacket.

He was not even sure why, at the last minute, he had slipped it on. Certainly, he was not afraid of a faceoff with Pete Fish. He was ten years younger and in much better physical condition than Pete. There really was no reason he should need this gun. Pete Fish certainly never carried a gun, as far as he knew.

Then he thought of Thomas and smiled. *He* at least would be pleased. Thomas thought the revolver had a power of its own, one that had nothing to do with bullets, and he was not the only one. Just the other day at the barbeque, his old Aunt Annie Eagletree, who had chipped in to buy him the gun, asked about it in no uncertain terms. She could not imagine he would be out in public without that gun.

"In the old days a man always had a weapon about him." She moved her head slowly from side to side. "You never know when you will need to defend yourself or your family. My father kept a knife under his pillow every night of his life. Once I asked him, 'Azhe'e, what makes you keep that knife there for? It might pop open and cut your ear off sometime."

"What did he say about that." Charlie was grinning.

"He said, 'My father slept with a knife and his father did too! They never cut their ears off and both of them lived past eighty.' I couldn't argue with that."

Annie Eagletree was not to be dissuaded. "Are you wearing that gun we bought you?" She said this, though she could see he was in a T-shirt and would have been hard pressed to conceal a gun. She looked him up and down. "I see on TV where some cops wear their guns on the back of their belt inside their pants; some even keep one strapped to their lower leg under their trousers." She looked over the serving counter and down at his ankles to see if this might be the case. Billy Redhouse, who was in line behind her and was listening, looked over the counter as well.

Charlie had long ago given up trying to convince his aunt he wasn't really a cop.

"Yep, that's where I keep it all right. I can't show you right now. I don't want people to know where it's at, just in case." She gave him a conspiratorial wink and moved on, satisfied.

Billy Redhouse nodded as he received his helping of lamb, smiled, and gave him a thumbs up.

It was all Charlie could do to keep a straight face. Aunt Annie was his favorite of his mother's sisters. He knew the gun set the family back a good amount, should you factor in the turquoise work. He tried to wear it when he went to visit one or the other of them. The men would nod sagely and lift an eyebrow at one another, indicating with their lips the location of the hidden gun. The stories of his expertise with the weapon had grown by leaps and bounds after the Patsy Greyhorse case, at least among the family. They were all very proud of him.

~~~~~~~

Pete Fish was sitting in his new SUV when Charlie pulled in, and he motioned him over.

Charlie grabbed a jacket and a cap that said NAVAJO PRIDE on the front and hurried across the lot. Pete Fish must be in a big hurry this morning, Charlie mused as he thought they were ahead of schedule. He hoped to see Sue and check his phone messages.

Sue Hanagarni watched nervously from the office window as

the two men drove off. She thought Charlie would at least stop by before he left. She knew Pete Fish had a two-way radio in his vehicle, but her repeated attempts to contact him went unanswered. He must have the radio turned off, she thought. Charlie would have picked up the mike when he heard her voice even if Pete had been too busy. She would try them again later in the morning and hoped to catch them before they dropped out of range. Certain areas on the reservation were "black holes" when it came to communications.

Pete Fish seemed preoccupied as he pulled out of the parking lot and pointed the Suburban west on US 64. His hands trembled slightly as he adjusted the rearview mirror. He had not spoken a single word of greeting, just turned up the volume on the radio station, then adjusted the squelch on the two-way to silence it. Charlie took this as a foreshadowing of things to come and kept his thoughts to himself. Pete's eyes were hidden by sunglasses. His lips moved, but silently, and not in sync with the radio's music. A slight sweat had broken out on his brow, and he wiped it occasionally on his shirtsleeve.

They reached the Arizona state line in less than thirty minutes and soon after veered left on 160. Pete pulled into the trading post at Mexican Water and sat a long moment staring, as though in a daze, at the long, white building.

"Let's get something to drink," he said finally. Not waiting for an answer, he climbed down from the SUV and, without looking back, went into the store.

Charlie looked after him, thinking at first he would just stay in the car but then changed his mind.

Inside the store he spotted Pete Fish just coming out of the restroom. Charlie turned to the refrigerated cases of cold drinks and selected two bottles of water then a soda, which he opened and took a long, slow swallow, causing the carbonation to burn all the way down and make his eyes water. Pete came up behind him and chose a soda but no water.

"I'm Hungry."

Charlie agreed with a nod and pointed to a selection of burritos that could be heated in the microwave oven which sat beneath a huge arrow painted on the wall, indicating the appliance. The proprietor had apparently grown weary of pointing out the obvious.

Pete removed his dark glasses to read the labels, and Charlie was taken aback at his hollow bloodshot eyes. Pete seemed unable to focus in the fluorescent light of the store and moved several packages back and forth in front of his eyes. Finally, he seemed to give up and just went with whatever he had in his hand.

"I could go for one of those breakfast burritos myself," Charlie said, keeping one eye on Pete, who moved over to the microwave without comment.

After the two men heated their food, Pete Fish turned to the counter, where he paid only for himself before moving to the door without a backward glance. Charlie hadn't expected Pete to pay for his; he had always been tight of pocket, usually the last one in line at the cash register in hopes someone else would pick up the tab. Charlie was surprised he had not lagged behind this time, proving once again, Pete Fish's mind was somewhere else.

Back in the Suburban, Charlie stowed his bottles of water in the door pocket and began unwrapping his burrito. Pete had already crammed half of his down and, with eyes watering from the green chilies, gulped down a long swallow of soda.

"Hard to believe, maybe," Pete said, still choking a little, "but I was born only a few miles from here." He waved a hand at the desolate scenery as he took another bite.

"Do you get back much?" Charlie didn't really care, but the answer surprised him.

"I've never been back—not since I was sixteen anyway. I went to the mission school when I was eight, then boarding school, and then the university."

"Didn't even go home during the summers?"

"Home wasn't much," Pete said, cleaning up a few crumbs. "I liked school. I guess I was about the only kid who did."

"Are any of your people still here?"

Pete Fish just nodded his head and started the car.

"They're here."

At Tes Nez La' Pete turned the big Chevrolet north on a little used dirt track.

"So are you going to tell me what we're doing up here?" Charlie had waited long enough and thought it was time for a few answers.

"You'll see soon enough. Just sit back and relax. You don't get to see something like this every day."

See what? Charlie thought but left it unsaid. He could see Pete Fish drifting off again to some other time and place.

They were well off the highway when the Suburban made one final turn to the west and began a steep ascent toward a long hogback ridge. The rocky track was probably an old access trail to some forgotten camp or maybe a woodcutter's road that had run out of wood. The Suburban pitched side to side and occasionally bounced the frame off the shelving rock. Charlie was glad it wasn't his truck.

Finally, at the top of the ridge the trail leveled out as it angled off across a narrow mesa at the end of the hogback. It ended at a promontory overlooking several hundred square miles of reservation. It was quite a drop—straight down, as far as Charlie could see.

Pete Fish stopped the car and turned to him, an expression akin to disbelief on his face. "I have now come full circle," he said pointing to a mound of rotted cedar logs and adobe mud just back from the rim. "I was born right in that hogan." He got out and moved to the front of the car to relieve himself on a small bush.

Charlie felt now as though he were watching a poorly directed movie, one that would likely have a bad ending. He freed the .38 from its holster and moved it to the side pocket, then taking a bit of toothpick from his burrito wrapper, jammed open the transmit button on the two-way radio. He watched as Pete Fish walked unsteadily to the edge of the rim and stood there, looking over the edge as if examining something. Apparently satisfied, he returned to the car and sat a moment dead still, staring into some parallel universe known only to himself. Finally, he turned in his seat and moved his chin to the west.

"There's a little spring that bubbles up out of the rocks," he pointed beyond the ruined dwelling, "just over there. My father said no one had ever seen a spring up this high...but as you can see..." he pointed at a little green bit of foliage beyond the ruined dwelling. "He thought this a sacred place because of that water. He wouldn't leave, no matter what. The place would only support a few head of stock. They both would have slowly starved to death living here."

"So did they finally move away?"

"Oh no...they didn't move away. He wouldn't leave." Pete Fish rubbed his chin. "I came back when I was sixteen...walled them up in a crack in the cliff down below. There wasn't a single piece of turquoise to put with them, except his ring...and I took it with me." He grimaced. "My father called it his 'lucky ring' and always said someday it would be mine."

"So they finally died then. That must have been awful for you to find them that way."

"No, they weren't dead when I found them. They were still hanging on, living as though nothing was wrong, hardly able to make it to the spring each day. No one even knew they were up here. They were too proud to ask for help." A single tear trickled down Pete Fish's cheek. Charlie would not have thought him capable of tears, but there it was. "I couldn't leave them here like that."

"Pete…do you mean you killed your own people here?"

"You do understand, I couldn't just leave them out here like that," he flicked the tear away, "with me away at school trying to study, make a new life and all. No, I couldn't have stood that. It was better they be safe, so I didn't have to worry about them so much." He brushed a sleeve across his eyes and nearly smiled. "You probably thought I brought you out here to do you some harm too, didn't you?"

"It crossed my mind."

Pete peered thoughtfully through the windshield across the far expanses of barren country.

"Sue would never marry me, would she, even if you were out of the way?"

"No Pete, she would not. We are going to be married soon." Charlie shook his head and forged on. "Sue would not have gone with you, no matter what happened." He knew now he was treading on dangerous ground.

Pete Fish sighed and looked away. "That's what I thought. I had planned to kill you but then finally realized it wouldn't get me what I really wanted." He raised a large caliber pistol from the driver side pocket and swung it to cover Charlie, who threw up his left arm like a chicken's wing.

"I didn't bring you out here to kill you, Charlie; I brought you out here to kill me. I've thought about it a great deal, and I think this would be best in the long run. I'll get more satisfaction out of it this way.

"Pete, let's go back to town. You need to get some help," Charlie whispered.

"You don't understand, Charlie. I wouldn't have any problem killing you. I could have made a lot of money, in fact, killing you." He looked Charlie square in the eye. "But that money wouldn't mean anything. I know that now. My peace must be made right here." He made a little motion with the muzzle of the gun. "I will only kill you if you make me." He blinked his eyes several times as though trying to clear his mind. "I want you to suffer Charlie, the way you have made me suffer. I want you to have this on your conscience for the rest of your life. It will be my revenge and, in the end, maybe even my salvation."

Charlie edged toward the door. "Now Pete, you need to get hold of yourself. This is crazy talk!" His right hand was hidden at his side, clutching the .38 tucked safely away in the side pocket. He was already easing it to his side when he heard the cold, hard click.

Pete Fish thumbed the hammer back on the big automatic and leveled it at Charlie's head. "What say, boy?"

Charlie's revolver fired almost of itself right across his belly. He felt the concussion clear to his backbone. There was no aiming or hope of accurately placing a shot. He wasn't even aware he had pulled the trigger. It was all instinct, and the will of the little revolver to do what it was designed to do—shoot someone in the belly at very close range.

Pete Fish should not have been surprised, but he looked surprised nonetheless. No matter how much you expect it, getting shot in the belly is always a surprise. It instantly sickens one, like a kick in the private parts. Reflex alone caused Pete Fish to pull his own gun's trigger. The .45 slug exploded past Charlie and through the side window, taking a small piece of Charlie's ear with it. It was that close. Pete Fish was still alive, but the fight had gone out of him, being shot in the belly and all. The gun dropped from his fingers, and he gripped the steering wheel with both hands. One might have thought him barely wounded, should they not understand how these things work.

A .38 makes a nice, neat little hole going in but seldom has enough power to exit a man like Pete Fish. The gut then slips a little and seals the hole. Belly fat alone may plug it up almost instantly. Many times there is hardly even any blood, and bystanders commonly think the person was not hit at all.

Law enforcement officers, at one time, carried .38 caliber revolvers almost exclusively. After the movie *Dirty Harry* came out, however, they all got bigger guns. They could see the advantage then in having a hole on both sides of a person when they shot him.

These were just some of the thoughts running through Charlie's head as he opened the car door. He could feel blood oozing down the side of his own face. He was deaf since the muzzle blast but figured if he was still able to think and move, he must not be too bad. He pulled a handkerchief out of his pocket with his left hand and pressed it against the side of his head. He tightened his grip on the .38 with the other and kept a sharp eye on Pete Fish, who didn't appear to be getting any worse.

Charlie reached over and took the keys, then turned the squelch down on the two-way and un-keyed the microphone. There was instant chaos on the air, static, and the squeal of feedback from everyone opening their mike at the same time. "Well, that's good," Charlie said under his breath. "Some of what just happened may have got out."

Almost immediately dispatch broke through urgently demanding his "20." Charlie pinpointed his location as closely as he could and told them they had better send in Medivac out of Farmington. This ridge shouldn't be too hard to find from the air.

He walked unsteadily around to the other side of the car and asked Pete Fish if there was anything he could do for him until the chopper got there. Pete squinted and blinked several times. It was hard for him to say very much. "Water!" was all he finally managed.

Charlie retrieved a water bottle and tried to give him a little sip. Pete shook his head, indicating the spring with a wave of his hand.

Charlie sighed and emptied out the bottle. The greenery around the spring was easy to see, and the old path from the ruined *hogan* was plain even after all these years. It wouldn't hurt to humor Pete Fish a little bit. He doubted this sacred spring water would allow him to jump up and run off. He could see where someone, many years before, had hollowed out a little basin now filled with clear, cold water. In this harsh, dry land, where water is life, he could imagine how someone might think this spring a miracle. When he returned to the car, Pete Fish was sitting up a bit straighter, and Charlie gave him just a sip of the spring water. Pete smiled then, and Charlie knew he had done the right thing.

Charlie thought to himself, "That water must taste just as it did when he was a boy."

~~~~~~~

In the hospital, Charlie was treated, then after showing his badge, was allowed to hang around waiting for the surgeons report on Pete Fish. Word was a long time coming, but three hours later, when the doctor finally did come out, he seemed pleased and noted what a lucky man Pete was. The damage might have been irreparable left untreated even a few minutes more. Now, however, there was a good chance he might recover. Pete was, in fact, already conscious. Charlie went in with two federal investigators, who also had been waiting.

The investigators quickly convinced Pete Fish the transmitted radio conversation alone was enough to send him away. They reminded him too there was no statute of limitations on the long-ago murder of his parents. In the end, with nothing more to lose, Pete Fish confessed all and, in the process, implicated Councilmen Donald Benally and Robert Ashki in the plot to murder government witnesses. They too would now be key figures in the ongoing Grand Jury conspiracy indictments.

Sue arrived earlier and was still waiting for Charlie. It was chaos at work, and reports on his condition were so widely conflicting she wasn't sure what to expect when she finally saw him. Charlie tried to call several times, but the switchboard had been jammed with traffic, and he could not get through.

Later, as Sue drove Charlie home, he told her everything. He almost felt sorry for Pete Fish. He heard a lot of sad stories on the reservation, he said, but few sadder than that.

"I guess so," Sue murmured. "It's kinda hard for me to feel sorry for someone who killed his own parents though."

"Well, you know, it was once very common among the people. When it was time to move camp, and the old people were too frail or sick to go along, then they were often just left with a little food and fire. The family just left them behind. The old people expected it too. It had always been that way. It was for the good of the family. When it was time to follow the game or move quickly to avoid enemies, there was no recourse. Remember, this was in the olden times before horses and social security." Charlie was just rambling on now, enjoying the ride with Sue and looking forward to what he hoped would be a pleasant afternoon.

"But still, in this day and age, you would have to be off your rocker to do such a thing," Sue insisted.

Charlie touched his bandaged ear. "I know. I suppose there's a limit to what you can forgive in a person these days."

"Speaking of that," Sue arched her eyebrows at him, "I heard you say on the radio that we were getting married soon." She smiled her serious smile. "It may have just slipped my mind, but I don't recall you asking."

Charlie flew into a fit of coughing and, finally, with watering eyes, he said, "I was going to ask you tonight when we were out to dinner in town." And when that got no response, "You did remember we were going out to dinner tonight, didn't you?"

"So you figured you better tell Pete Fish first, huh?"

"It seemed an opportune moment, what with him wondering should he just kill me and hang around to marry you himself. I thought I better nip that in the bud."

"Nip it? Well, there are about 30 people who heard you say it.

It's going to be pretty hard to get out of now."

"I don't want to get out of it." There was a light buzzing in his bandaged ear. He hoped his hearing was coming back. "I meant what I said." Charlie turned to the window, and she could barely make out his next words. "At the time, I thought it might be the last chance I would have to let you know how I feel."

Sue watched a small dust devil whirling its way across the road. She slowed slightly to miss it, then turned to Charlie and said softly, "Well, I suppose that's about the most romantic thing I've ever heard you say." Her smile caused a small flutter in his heart. He closed his eyes and let his thoughts drift off to that little place in the country and how he was going to make a corral for his new horse. He would find a horse for Sue. Horses just seem to do better when there are two. Pretty much like people.

Sue glanced over at Charlie as he nodded off. She thought they would do well together. It was time they moved forward in life—together.

~~~~~~

Aida Marie Winters rose that morning to a brilliant pink glow across the eastern horizon and went to feed the horses. Charlie and Thomas said they would be bringing them about mid-morning At last she would see Sally's children. *Possibly the first and last time she would ever see them,* she thought. *It wasn't Sally's fault; she never even learned to drive a car and was, in many ways, like a child herself. Well, at least her children would have better opportunities.* Aida had seen to that.

She would take the children up the hill behind the house to see their mother's grave. She figured they were too young to have picked up the Navajo distaste for death, especially considering all the time they had spent with the *Ute*, who had no particular aversion to it—at least not the ones they had been around. She would let the children place fresh flowers on the grave if they liked. Some of those flowers were perennial, planted years ago by Sally Klee herself. It was fitting her children should carry them to her.

Aida remembered too what Sally had mentioned to her when she first came there. It was a thing Aida now thought Thomas should know. Caleb had been born after Freddie Chee ordered Thomas to leave, so there was something he never knew—Caleb's middle name. Even Caleb didn't know it. Sally had not wanted either of them to know it at the time. Thomas had asked both Caleb and his sister what the boy's middle name was. Both told him they didn't think he had one.

It was Thomas—his name was Caleb Thomas Begay.

Aida, not one to dwell long in sorrow, soon recalled Charlie's phone call of the night before, causing her to brighten considerably. She contemplated Robert Ashki and Donald Benally sitting in jail this fine morning, awaiting a bail hearing that was not likely to bring any relief. It occurred to her that maybe there was justice in the world after all.

Charlie told her there were now four tribal councilmen who would likely not see the light of day for a while. "In fact," he said, "Thomas's Uncle John Nez is already thinking of running for Ashki's seat on the council. His friend Marissa convinced him he would be a shoo-in to run in their district." He went on to say, "White women are known to be quite aggressive when it comes to righting wrongs, political or otherwise." Aida could almost see him grin over the phone. She knew he was referring to her, and this made her grin too.

The world was changing, that was for certain, and she was glad she was still around to see it, maybe even help it along a little.

~~~~~~~~~

Aida was sitting on the front porch scanning the horizon when Thomas finally drove his big Dodge truck up the lane. There was a two-horse trailer on behind which bore a tribal insignia. She could see Charlie in the passenger seat and two little faces peering out between them. Aida smiled softly and went to greet them.

Maybe Thomas would let the children come visit for a few weeks each summer. These children could have a place in everyone's future. Little did she know how prophetic that thought was.

The dusk of one story is often the dawn of another and, like the dawn, brings fresh beginnings.

ABOUT THE AUTHOR

The Author and his wife spend most winters in Mexico and summers at home in Colorado where he pursues an active interest in the pre-history of the region. He welcomes reader comments at: rachappell@yahoo.com

If you've enjoyed this book, please go to its Amazon book page or http://www.amazon.com/ebook/dp/B00BOZ3WH8 and leave a short review. It would be most appreciated.

Glossary

Ashiihi – Salt People (clan) *

Atsili – Younger brother

Anasazi – Pueblo ancestors

Azhe'e – Father

Billigaana – White people

Chindi (or chinde) – Spirit of the dead *

Da dichin' ninizen? – *A*re you hungry?

Dinè – Navajo people

Dinè Bikeyah – Navajo country

Gah' – Rabbit

Hataalii – Shaman (Singer)*

Hastiin (Hosteen) – Man

Hogan – Traditional dwelling

Hozo – To walk in beauty *

Shahastoi – Uncle*

Tse' Bita'I – Shiprock

Yaa' eh t'eeh – Greeting - Hello

Yeenaaldiooshii – Skinwalker, witch*

Ye'i – Spirit-helper*

Notes

1. *Ashiihi – The Salt People are thought to be the most numerous clan affiliation in the Navajo Mountain area. Old White Man Killer was an early and powerful Salt People clan resident of the area, coming there in 1892. He is thought to have many descendants.

6. *Chindi – When a person dies inside a hogan, it is said that his chindi or spirit remains there forever, causing the hogan to be abandoned. Chindi are not considered benevolent entities. For the traditional Navajo, just speaking a dead person's name may call up his chindi and cause harm to the speaker.

11. *Hataalii – Generally known as a "Singer" among the Dinè, these men are considered "Holy Men" and have apprenticed to older practitioners—sometimes for many years—to learn the ceremonies. They make the sand-paintings that are an integral part of the healing and know the many songs which must be sung in the correct order.

14. *Hozo – For the Navajo "hozo" (sometimes hozoji) is a general state of well-being, both physical and spiritual, that indicates a certain "state of grace" which is referred to as "walking in beauty." Illness or depression are the usual cause of "loss of hozo," which puts one out of sync with the people as a whole. There are ceremonies to restore hozo and return the ailing person to a oneness with his people.

15. *Shahastoi – Elder man or distant Uncle – In the Navajo culture there is a term for nearly any relationship to avoid the use of the persons actual name when addressing him (considered bad manners by a traditional Navajo).

(Continued)

18. *Yeenaaldiooshii – These witches, as they are often referred to, are the chief source of evil or fear in the traditional Navajo super-stitions. They are thought to be capable of many unnatural acts, such as flying, or turning themselves into werewolves and other ethereal creatures; hence the term Skinwalkers, referring to their ability to change forms or skins.

19. *Ye'i – A generally benevolent spirit-helper, often seen depict-ed in weavings and sand-paintings. At major "Sings" or ceremo-nies, men dressed as ye'i's go among the crowd as helper-beggars and provide a valuable service to the Hataalii performing the cere-mony.

Made in the USA
Middletown, DE
03 April 2019